MARGARET K. McELDERRY BOOKS
An imprint of Simon & Schuster Children's Publishing Division
1230 Avenue of the Americas, New York, New York 10020
This book is a work of fiction. Any references to historical events, real people, or real locales are used fictitiously. Other names, characters, places, and incidents are the product of the author's imagination, and any resemblance to actual events or locales or persons, living or dead, is entirely coincidental.
Copyright © 2004 by Ellen Hopkins
All rights reserved, including the right of reproduction
in whole or in part in any form.
MARGARET K. McELDERRY BOOKS is a trademark of Simon & Schuster, Inc.
For information about special discounts for bulk purchases,
please contact Simon & Schuster Special Sales at 1-866-506-1949
or business@simonandschuster.com.The Simon & Schuster Speakers Bureau can bring authors to your live event. For more information or to book an event, contact the Simon & Schuster Speakers Bureau at 1-866-248-3049 or visit our website at www.simonspeakers.com.
Book design by Sammy Yuen Jr.
The text of this book was set in Trade Gothic Condensed.
Manufactured in the United States of America
First paperbook edition October 2004
35 34 33 32 31
Library of Congress Control Number 2003116437
ISBN 978-0-689-86519-0
ISBN 978-1-4391-0651-8 (eBook)

DEDICATION

This book is dedicated to my family, and all families whose lives have been touched by the monster.

With special thanks to Lin Oliver and Steve Mooser and their wonderful SCBWI, which guided my way.

AUTHOR'S NOTE

While this work is fiction, it is loosely based on a very true story—my daughter's. The monster did touch her life, and the lives of her family. My family. It is hard to watch someone you love fall so deeply under the spell of a substance that turns him or her into a stranger. Someone you don't even want to know.

Nothing in this story is impossible. Much of it happened to us, or to families like ours. Many of the characters are composites of real people. If they ring true, they should. The "baby" at the end of the book is now seven years old, and my husband and I have adopted him. He is thriving now, but it took a lot of extra love.

If this story speaks to you, I have accomplished what I set out to do. Crank is, indeed, a monster—one that is tough to leave behind once you invite it into your life. Think twice. Then think again.

Flirtin' with the Monster

Life was good
before I
met

the monster.

After,
life

was great.

At
least

for a little while.

Introduction

So you want to know all
about me. Who

            I am.

What chance meeting of
brush and canvas painted

            the face

you see? What made
me despise the girl

            in the mirror

enough to transform her,
turn her into a stranger,

            only not.

So you want to hear
the whole story. Why

            I swerved

off the high road,
hard left to nowhere,

            recklessly

indifferent to those
coughing my dust,

            picked up speed

no limits, no top end,
just a high velocity rush

to madness.

lone

everything changes.
Some might call it distorted reality,
but it's exactly the place I need to be:

     no mom,
               Marie, ever more distant,
               in her midlife quest for fame
     no stepfather,
               Scott, stern and heavy-handed
               with unattainable expectations
     no big sister,
               Leigh, caught up in a tempest
               of uncertain sexuality
     no little brother,
               Jake, spoiled and shameless
               in his thievery of my niche.

Alone,

     there is only the person inside.
     I've grown to like her better
     than the stuck-up husk of me. She's

not quite silent,
>   shouts obscenities just because
>   they roll so well off the tongue
not quite straight-A,
>   but talented in oh-so-many
>   enviable ways
not quite sanitary,
>   farts with gusto, picks
>   her nose, spits like a guy
not quite sane,
>   sometimes, to tell you the truth,
>   even *I* wonder about her.

Alone,

> there is no perfect daughter,
> no gifted high-school junior,
> no Kristina Georgia Snow.
>   There is only Bree.

n Bree

I suppose
she's always been
there, vague as a soft
copper pulse of moonlight
through blossoming seacoast

                                        fog.

I wonder
when I first noticed
her, slipping in and out
of my pores, hide-and-seek
spider in fieldstone, red-bellied

                                        phantom.

I summon
Bree when dreams
no longer satisfy, when
gentle clouds of monotony
smother thunder, when Kristina

                                        cries.

I remember
the night I first
let her go, opened the
smeared glass, one thin pane,
cellophane between rules and sin,

                                        freed.

ore on Bree

Spare me
those Psych '01 labels,
I'm no more schizo than most.

Bree is
no imaginary playmate,
no overactive pituitary,
no alter ego, moving in.
Hers is the face I wear,

                    treading the riptide,

fathomless oceans where

                good girls drown.

Besides,
even good girls have secrets,
ones even their best friends must guess.

Who do
they turn to on lonely
moon-shadowed sidewalks?
I'd love to hear them confess:
Who do they become when

night descends,

a cool puff of smoke, and

vampires come out to party?

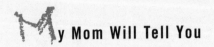y Mom Will Tell You

it started with a court-ordered visit.

> *The judge had a God complex.*

I guess for once she's right.
Was it just last summer?

> *He started an avalanche.*

My mom enjoys discussing
her daughter's downhill slide.

> *It swallowed her whole.*

I still wore pleated skirts, lipgloss.
Crooked bangs defined my style.

> *Could I have saved her?*

My mom often outlines her first
marriage, its bitter amen. Interested?

> *I was too young, clueless.*

I hadn't seen Dad in eight years.
No calls. No cards. No presents.

> *He was a self-serving bastard.*

My mom, warrior goddess, threw
down the gauntlet when he phoned.

> *He played the prodigal trump card.*

I begged. Pouted. Plotted. Cajoled.
I was six again, adoring Daddy.

> *What the hell gave him that right?*

My mom gave a detailed run-down
of his varied bad habits.

Contrite was not his style.

I promised. Swore. Crossed my heart.
Recited the D.A.R.E. pledge verbatim.

How could she love him so much?

My mom relented, kissed me
good-bye, sad her perfume.

Things would never be the same.

I think it was the last time she kissed me.
But I was on my way to Daddy.

Aboard United 1425

The flight attendant escorted me to
a seat beside a moth-munched toupee.
Yellowed dentures clacked cheerfully,
suggested I make myself comfy.

> *Three hours is a mighty long time.*

Three hours is a long time, astraddle
a 747's wing, banshee engines
screaming, earachy babies fussing,
elderly seatmate complaining.

> *Can't stand flying.*
> *Makes me nauseous.*

I get nauseous when vid screens
play movies I've seen three times,
seat belt signs deny pee breaks
and first class smells like real food.

> *Pretzels?*
> *For this ticket price?*

For the price, I'd expect Albert to
tone down the gripe machine. I closed
my eyes, tried to shut him out, but second
run movies can't equal conversation.

> *My wife died last year.*
> *Been alone since.*

I've been alone since my mom met Scott.
He sucked the nectar from her heart
like a famished butterfly. No nurture,
no nourishment left for Kristina.

> *A vacation is a poor substitute*
> *for love.*

Two Hours into the Flight

Albert snored, soft
as a hummingbird's
hover. His moody
smile suggested he'd
found his Genevieve,

     just beyond   time
     just beyond   space
     just beyond this   continuum.

I watched his face,
gentled by dreams,
until sun winks off
the polished fuselage
hypnotized me,

     not quite   asleep
     not quite   conscious
     not quite in this   dimension.

I coasted along a
byway, memory,
glimpses of truth
speed bumps
within childish
belief,

        almost   ultimate
        almost   reliable
        almost total   insanity.

Daddy waited
in the dead-end
circle, reaching
out for me.
I couldn't

        find his   embrace
        find his   answers
        find his excuse for   tears.

Faster. Faster.
He'd waited too
many years for
me to come looking.
Hadn't he? I

        needed to   see
        needed to   know
        needed a lot   more.

Hot Landing

Hot runway.
Hot brakes.
Hot desert sand
outside the window,
wind-sculpted crystalline
slivers, reflecting a new
summer's sun.

Good-bye, young lady.

Good-bye, Albert.

Good-bye, toupee.
Good-bye, dentures.
Good-bye, in-flight
glimpses of a soul,
aching, and dreams,
fractured, injuries only
death could cure.

Have a nice vacation.

You too.

You relax.
You pretend to have fun.
You share a toast with me:
here's to seasonal
madness, part-time
relatives and
substitutes for love.

The Prince of Albuquerque

June is pleasant in Reno,
kind of breezy and all.
I boarded the plane in
clingy jeans and a
long-sleeved T. Black.

It's a whole lot hotter in Albuquerque.

I wobbled up the skywalk,
balancing heavy twin carry-ons.
Fingers of sweat grabbed
my hair and pressed it
against my face.

No one seemed to notice.

I scanned the crowd at the gate.
Too tall. Not tall enough.
Too old. Way too old.
There, with the sable hair,
much like my own.

How was it possible?

I thought he was much better
looking, the impression
of a seven-year-old whose
daddy was the Prince
of Albuquerque.

I melted, sleet on New Mexico asphalt.

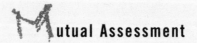utual Assessment

Daddy watched the gate, listing
a bit as he hummed a bedtime
tune, withdrawn from who knows
which memory bank.

       "Daddy?"   *Roses are red, my love.*

He overlooked me like sky
above a patch of dirt,
and I realized he, too, searched
for a face suspended in yesterday.

       "It's me."   *Violets are blu-oo-oo.*

Peculiar eyes, blue-speckled
green like extravagant eggs,
met my own pale aquamarine.
Assessing. Doubt gnawing.

       "Hey."   *Sugar is . . . Kristina?*

He hugged me, too tightly. Nasty
odors gulped. Marlboros. Jack
Daniels. Straightforward B.O.
Not like Scott's ever-clean smell.

I can't believe how
much you've grown!

"It's been eight
years, Dad."

From daddy to dad
in thirty seconds. We were
strangers, after all.

Got in a Car with a Stranger

A '92 Geo, pink under
primer, not quite a
princely coach. Dad and
I attempted small talk.

> *How's your sister?*

"Gay."

Sequestered on a California
campus. When she outed,
I cringed. Mom cried.
You called her queer.

> *How's your mother?*

"Older."

Prettier, gift-wrapped
in 40ish self-esteem, a
wannabe writer and workout
fanatic, sweating ice.

> *How's what's-his-name?*

"Indifferent."

Either that or flat in my
face, yet oddly always
there exactly when I
need him. Unlike you.

              And how are you?
    "Okay."

Near-sighted. Hormonal.
Three zits monthly.
Often confused.
Lusting for love.
        "You?"
              Same.

Small Talk Shrank to Minuscule

Hot? Not! Wait till August!

The carriage burped. Screeched.
Hiccupped. I tightened my seat-belt,
like that could save me.

Straight A's, huh? Got your brains
from your old man.

I was starting to doubt it.
No air-con, windows down,
oil flavored the air.
Conversation took an ugly turn.

Never been laid? Tell the truth
little girl.

Like it was his business. He
reached for his Marlboros, took
one, offered the pack. My lip
curled. He lit up anyway.

Quit once. Your mother bitched
me out of the habit.

I watched him inhale, blow
smoke signals. Exhale. Beyond
the ochre haze, city turned to
suburbs. Not pretty suburbs.

> *She was the bitch queen. I started*
> *again soon as I moved out.*

The Geo limped into
a weather-chewed parking
lot. I escaped the front
seat. Aired out in blistering heat.

> *Here we are. Home sweet home.*
> *What's mine is yours.*

I'd made an awful mistake.
Daddy wasn't the Prince of
Albuquerque. He was the King of Cliché.

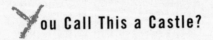ou Call This a Castle?

Cracked cement ramparts,
  a less than mighty bastion,
    swamp cooler overflow,
       drool down the battlement.
      Behind the stockade walls,
       faceless generals barked
         orders to their private troops,
         drilled their little soldiers.

Welcome to my castle.

You call this a castle?
Heat throbbing off the
parking lot convinced me
to chance crumbling stairs.
And there, step four, flight two,
I bumped into my White Knight.
Okay, maybe more like gray.
I'll compromise with silver.

Not My Type

No shirt

      hot bod.
      His, that is.
      So why did
      I break out in
      a sweat?

No shoes

      barefoot,
      bare chest, with
      a bare, baby face
      to make the
      angels sing.

Nothing

      but ragged
      cut-offs,
      hugging a
      tawny six pack,
      and a smile.

No pin-up
          pretty boy
          could touch,
          a smile that
          zapped every cell.
          He was definitely

not my type.

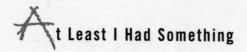t Least I Had Something

to think about
besides my dad's
less than palatial
apartment.

If he qualified
as royalty in this true
blue collar
kingdom,

I had zero desire
to see how the
working class
lived.

Dad Had to Go to Work

Work?

> You've heard of work.

You couldn't take
one day off?

> You don't know my boss.

Does he know
about me?

> She knows you're here.

Your daughter
comes to visit . . .

> She doesn't know.

Know what?

> That you're my daughter.

Who am I, then?

> A long-lost relative.

He Worked in a Bowling Alley

Under the table,
so I don't screw
up my disability.

Unsticking stuck
balls, fitting stinky
shoes, collecting
cash from the crop
du jour of the
great unwashed.

No one there's
gonna tell. They
got their own secrets,

No worries about
bubblegum, athlete's
foot, or the current
flu, passed bill to
bill, ball to ball,
shoe to shoe.

Like who's making
out in the back room,
who's striking out.

Geo unlocked
in a parking lot
where the color of
your jacket might
mean your life, wrong
night, wrong time.

> *It's not the best*
> *neighborhood, but*
> *hey, come along.*

Opted Out

Long trip,
long day,
no thanks,
I'll stay.

Okay.

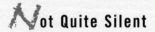ot Quite Silent

The empty boxes
Dad imagined
rooms.

Glurp . . . glurp . . . glurp

Hot drops into
deep kitchen
stainless.

Plunk . . . . plunk

Cool drips on
chipped bathroom
porcelain.

Chh-ka-chh

Sleepy branches
scratching bedroom
glass.

You crazy sonofabitch!

Neighbors through
thin plaster
walls.

The Screaming

flashed   me   back

to   a   time

when   Mom   and   Dad

were   still   together

if   you   could   call

miles   apart   together.

Leigh and I would huddle close
under the blankets, whispering,
as if the whispers of two little girls
could blot out the barrage of hateful words
beyond our bedroom's thin plaster walls.
Dad's vicious slurred epithets came through
too loud and too clear.

But it is Mom's low, level threats I best remember.

You do not deserve these children and when I'm through with you in court you'll be lucky to get visitation.

She was right.
And I still had not forgiven her.
Maybe he wasn't perfect.
But he was still my dad.

Of Course, When I Was Little

I didn't understand the
terminology of words like

        infidelity.

Nor the implications
of my father's sundry

        addictions.

I only knew my wicked
mother took us far away,

        kept us far apart.

Time passed, with little
word from Dad.

But, having experienced
Mom's growing

        frustration

at a stalled career and
family life's daily

        limitations

I put the blame squarely
on her. As for Dad,

        I could have forgiven

him pretty much anything,
even his silence.

As long as I could forever
stay his little princess.

Okay, Over the Last Few Years

I may have gained a little perspective.

Mom struggled to raise two kids

on her own, at least until Scott

blundered into her life.

Jake was a late addition,
one the workout queen accepted

and loved despite killer stretch marks
and sure-to-sag-even-more boobs.

As for Dad, well, truth be told, his love
of drugs surpassed his love of family.

And when we were small, he just
happened to install cable TV,
giving him every opportunity

to experience the wild side of
bored, stay-at-home housewives,
eager for entertainment.

So it was, perhaps, ironic
that I discovered . . .

Dad Hadn't Paid His Cable Bill

Three fuzzy channels
    hissed and spit
        a rerun of *Friends,*
            extra-inning baseball, and
                soap opera, en español.

I should have gone
    straight to bed,
        counted cracks
            in the ceiling.
                Instead, I went outside.

Cigarette smoke,
    toxic curls in the
        stairwell at my feet,
            soft voices rising,
                pheromone fog.

He was still there,
    my silver knight,
        flirting with some
            fallen Guinivere in
                short shorts and a cropped T.

I kept to the shadows,
        observing the game
            I hadn't dared play,
                absorbing the rules
                    with adhesive eyes.

The Rules

Uncomplicated, this
child's game.

> He says, *Please?*
>   She says, "Can't."
> He, *Why not?*
>   She, "I'm not that kind of a girl."

Then she spends twenty
minutes disproving
the theory, until

> Mother calls, *Hija?*
>   She answers, "Mama?"
> Mother, *Come inside now.*
>   She, "Be right there."

It's a lie. He pulls her
into his lap, silencing
meager protests with
full-lipped kisses.

He insists, *Now.*

        She resists, "Later."

He, *Promise?*

        She, "Cross my heart."

She Went Inside

I wasn't sure if I felt more
disappointed or relieved.
Guinivere really had him.

So I shouldn't want him.   Should I?
I didn't really want his perfect
pout, reaching hungrily
for my own timid lips.

I didn't have a clue how to   kiss.
Didn't really want his hands,
investigating the hills
and valleys of my landscape.

I'd never been touched by   a boy.
Didn't want his face,
burrowing into my hair,
finding my neck. Tasting.

I'd never even said hello to such   a complete stranger.
Didn't want his smoke,
making me gag, making me
want to taste something so gross.

It was all so confusing,   I mean,
I didn't want a boyfriend,
no summer fling to make
me want to stay in this alien place.

Anyway, I'd be speechless   if he asked.

Must Have Moaned

Hey.

He popped above the
stairs suddenly, a
wild-eyed Jack-in-the-box,
anticipating the
pay-off crank.

Oh, it's you.

Like he knew me,
knew I had no life,
suspected I'd come
spying, set up the game
just for me.

I waited for you.

I coughed a hello,
stamping sweaty
palm prints into not-so
wrinkle-free jeans.
Could he read minds?

I know what you're thinking.

Smile. Nod. Say
something witty
before he finds
out what an incredible
geek you are.

That you're too good for me.

He topped the staircase,
slinked closer, golden
eyes narrowing, reached
out and touched the flush
of my cheek.

But you're wrong.

49

The Wind Blew Up

My mind raced.
My heart joined in.
I shook my head,
mute as snowfall.

*What, then? Why do you look
at me that way?*

What could I say?
That some stranger
inside me couldn't
keep her eyes off him?

*I know you can talk. I heard
you before.*

I felt her stir, like a
breeze blowing up off
the evening sea. My
wind had awakened.

*You know, you're kind of cute,
in a stuck-up sort of way.*

She pumped through
my veins in hot, red
bursts. Blood pressure
rose in my face, blush.

You here for the summer? What's
your name?

Her tongue curled
easily behind my teeth,
and her words melted
between my lips.

"My friends call me Bree."

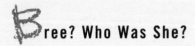

ree? Who Was She?

And where did that name
come from? I'd probably
heard it once in my life!

Pretty name, Bree.

Okay, good call.
Confidence flooded our
brain like hormones.
Our turn. Who was he?

My friends call me Buddy.

Hardly a handle
for a white knight.
Bree asked for the name
on his birth certificate.

Mom named me Adam.

Better. We liked it. So
why didn't he use it?
(Forgetting completely
about the Kristina thing.)

Hard name to live up to.

Not really. It isn't hard
to fall from grace. Revisit
Genesis. Maybe I'll go with
you. Might be fun.

You're a strange girl.

I had to agree. What
was up with this person,
Bree? And was she
a permanent fixture?

But I'd like to get to know you.

Wanted to Know Him, Too

Wanted to know
what Guinivere knew.

Bree might have pulled him
closer, tempted his kiss that very
moment, given hers in return.

But with a sudden slam, reality
kicked into gear. Downstairs,
Guinivere called his name.

     He answered,
          Up here.
I looked in his eyes, caught
a hint of warped humor,
jumped up to go inside.

     He asked,
          How long are you staying?
Not long enough, I wanted
to say. But I told him,
"Three weeks."

He said,
                Not much time.
Footsteps on the stairs.
Bree vanished, leaving
panic in her wake.

He finished,
                But maybe enough.

The Return of Guinivere

She took in the scene,
face cinder-block hard,
eyes blinking like
mad, black turn signals.

>"Who is she?"

As if he had something
to explain. He didn't,
did he? Yet his voice was
right beside my ear,

>*Bree.*

I swear I saw her claws
spring out. I froze, prey.
She told me her name was
Lince. Then translated,

>"Lynx."

She had claimed her territory.
I decided to let the wildcats
play, uninterrupted. His warm
hand whispered against mine.

>*See you soon.*

His promise fell,
soft as a premonition,
followed by the bobcat's
predatory growl,

"Me too."

That'll Teach Me

to spy
to moan
to covet

my neighbor's boyfriend.

I ran inside, tried

to breathe
to laugh
to silence

the drumming inside my head.

Went into the kitchen

to get a drink
to get away
to get a glimpse

of the biggest cockroach I'd ever seen.

Toss-and-Turn Night

Bone-oven hot outside,
swamp-cooler cool three
feet up the hallway,
temperature in Dad's
claustrophobic guest
room: lukewarm.

The bed was a monstrous box
spring. Thin, mildewed foam,
two sprays of Lysol, and one
thrift-store sheet were all
that lay between
Bedzilla and me.

Tried my right side. Kept
seeing the kitchen
cockroach, the one I
tried to pretend was
only a Mormon cricket,
Los Alamos–grown.

Tried my left side. Flashed
on my bedroom at home.
Pin clean, pretty in
mauve, a ballet of pink
butterflies on the walls,
pillow-top mattress to die for.

Flopped onto my back. Found
the keyhole behind my eyes,
squeezed through, into sleep.
Not slumber, but sleep just this
side of waking, where dreams
fuse with reality.

Through the Keyhole

I found myself in a meadow,
brilliant green beneath a soft
wash of sunshine.

I moved at a near sprint,
drawn toward a symphony,
primitive passion.

Lovemaking.

Wildcats mating, snarls at
the joining, satisfied roars
signaling completion.

I slowed, shifted upwind,
crept very near,
somehow unafraid.

Fascinated.

Some movement gave me
away. Exquisite feline eyes
found me in the grass,

golden eyes, flecked green.
He purred and she looked up.
I gasped at her face.

My face.

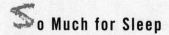So Much for Sleep

Jump-started awake,
I sat up in bed,
found the eyes of the lynx
at the glass, snarls
in the hallway.

Sweat-drenched,
shivering, I threw back
the sheet, went to the
window, three flights
above a deserted alley.

Found no eyes but dream eyes.

One demon conquered,
I slipped on flip-flops,
mediocre protection
against monster
cockroaches, wandered
toward the kitchen.

Found no snarls but Dad's snores.

Hid Out for Three Days

Spent them sleeping in,
like Dad.

> *I work late. No shame in that.*

Afternoons we ate fast
food and talked.

> *Sure I want more. Some day.*

He was pushing 45. Time
was running out.

> *A house of my own. A good woman.*

Surely he'd dated one or
two since Mom?

> *Slept with a few. Don't do movies. . . .*

There's more to dating
than movies.

> *Don't do dinner, unless they cook.*

Come on, Dad. What
about love?

> *Love is overrated. Besides . . .*

I couldn't believe
his confession:

> *No one can measure up to your mom.*

Even Spent Time at the Bowling Alley

Okay, I'd bowled before,
        averaged a solid 98, with one
                or two games around 130.
                But did you know some
        people spend half their lives
hanging out in bowling alleys?

        The same people arrived,
                around the same time
                        every night. It took
                        me three days to realize
                they came for more than just
        a few games of good, clean fun.

                Some came to flirt, obnoxious
                        in their efforts to make their
                                spouses jealous, or disregard
                                them altogether, desperate
                        to recapture escaped dreams and
                wasted years of youth.

Some came substance shopping,
        disappearing into back rooms
            and bathrooms, returning
                red-eyed and crusty-nosed,
            coughing and sniffling, too
    mellow or very, very wound up.

In school I was never confronted
        with drugs, surely never sought
            them out. But I wasn't exactly
            clueless. As I watched, one
        thing became obvious. Where
the party went, my dad followed.

He Hadn't Changed After All

But he wasn't such a bad guy,
really. Not ambitious, true.
In fact, you might call
him lazy, at least when
the drug of the day
was green.

> Been smokin' pot since I was 13,
> couldn't quit if I tried. Besides,
> why try? It keeps me happy,
> mellow. Makes me eat
> too much, but
> oh, well.

The white
stuff was a different
story. He'd stay up all
night, eating zip, bowling
and snorting line after line.
Rent money, right up the nose.

We used to
do coke, till "Just
Say No" put the stuff
out of reach. Now it's crank.
Meth. The monster. It's a bitch
on the body, but damn do you fly.

You Fly Until You Crash

Two
days,
two
nights,
no
sleep,
no
food,
come
down
off
the
monster,

you

crash

real

hard.

ad Crashed

Slept twelve hours, got
up for a drink and a
pee, slept six more.
Good thing it was his
day off.

But was it always his
day off? Or did he
sometimes go to work,
mind folded down
around exhaustion?

Did he sometimes
blow off work completely,
call in sick, notating on
his calendar the
Illness of the Day?

No bowling, no small talk,
just plain, empty time,
I walked down to
the corner store for
Pepsi and *Cosmopolitan*.

Guess who was buying
cigarettes, copper skin
glistening bittersweet
summer sweat. One
look, I was Play-Doh.

He Knew It, Too

He turned, flashed
a drop-dead-in-your-tracks
gorgeous grin.

Hey, Bree.

His voice dripped
honey and cream,
irresistible poison.

You been avoiding me?

I plead not guilty,
argued spending time
with my dad.

All-night bowling?

He knew too much. I
fumbled for change,
came up short.

No worries. My treat.

He paid for my Pepsi,
asked if he could
walk me back.

I'll be good. Honest.

Hip brushing hip,
his hand slipped
around my waist.

You on your own today?

Heartbeat bombs
went off in my head.
Spectacular.

Can we talk awhile?

is Mom Was at Work

We went to his apartment, a nice
        quiet place to talk awhile.
                Mind if I light up?

What could I say? It was his
        apartment.
                His lungs.
                        Bad habit, I know.

I watched hands, hard and etched
        like granite, light a match
                with finesse.
                        Do you have any bad habits?

I could have made up something.
        Instead I shook my head.
                Want any?

I wanted him. Bad enough. I reached
        for the cigarette in his hand.
                You don't smoke, do you?

I took a small puff. Struggled
        like hell not to cough.
            Or throw up.
                    Careful. You'll get sick.

So I did the sensible thing. Took
        another drag. Felt better.
                    Come here, Bree.

He pulled me close, locked my eyes,
        tilted his face just a fraction.
                Then I really felt queasy.

e Wanted to Kiss Me

I felt it with every nerve,
every fiber,
every molecule
of my being.

I wanted him to kiss me,
with every nerve,
every fiber,
every molecule
of my being.

But I was scared to kiss him.
Every nerve,
every fiber,
every molecule
screamed!

He leaned forward,
parted those
perfect lips.

At that exact moment,

every
single
thing
about
my
life
changed.

Forever.

First Kiss

They say you'll remember
your first kiss forever. I will.

It was Fourth of July.
It was Christmas.

Fireworks. Snowflakes.
Sunstroke and frostbite.

It was all that I could ask for
and completely unexpected.

> I expected demands.
> He gifted me with tenderness.
>
> I expected ego.
> He let me experiment.
>
> I expected disrespect.
> He called me beautiful.
>
> I expected him to expect perfection.
> He taught me all I needed to know.

The Week Flew By

Monday

> Ducked Lince and made out
> at the park.
> Learned a thing or three.

Tuesday

> Took in a movie.
> Sat in the back row.
> Really made out.

Wednesday

> Had a Slurpee fight.
> Kissed the sticky stuff
> off each other's faces.

Thursday

> Back to his apartment.
> Things got heavy.
> Heart-stomping heavy.

Friday

>Bummed a ride and went
>skinny-dipping up
>Red Rock Canyon.

Saturday

>Talked with Dad, wishing I was doing
>something else with Adam.
>Sneaked out after dinner
>for a smoke
>and a taste of tongue.

Sunday

>Met Adam at the bowling alley.

Somehow the Place Looked Different

What had changed?

It was still a run-down bowling
        alley in a bad part
            of town.

                I had changed.

Somehow I didn't care about
        other people's
            obsessions.

                I was obsessed.

Somehow I didn't care about
        public make-out
            sessions.

                I plotted make-out sessions.

Somehow I didn't care about
        women, stealing other
            women's boyfriends.

                Had I stolen someone's boyfriend?

Somehow I didn't care about
back-room parties.

It was my turn. I'd been invited.

Choices, Choices

Life is full of

choices.

We don't
always

make

good ones.
It seems to

Kristina

you gotta
be

crazy

to open your
windows,
invite the
demons in.

Bree

throws rocks
at the feeble
glass,

laughs.

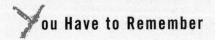You Have to Remember

It had been
a tempestuous week,
snared by emotions
rubbing me so raw
I hurt at night,

                alone in the dark.

I finagled my way
on this trip to fall back
in love with my dad.
Instead I fell
for a boy from

                the wrong side of the tracks,

worse, the wrong part
of the country! I
had come, wanting to
want to go home. Now the
dark side of Albuquerque

                looked pretty damn good.

So when he asked
about getting high, I didn't
think, I agreed. We smoked
some good California green.
Took three tries to put me in
                    the place he said I should be.
Sleepy. Not "high" at
all, but real low. And real
slow. Not my idea of a party,
except the munchies part. I
wanted to meet the monster.

                    Why go down if you can go up?

We Met at the Bowling Alley

I introduced Adam to my dad. He
and Buddy already knew each other.

Small building, you know.

Their networking surprised me.
Not exactly sure why.

Some good green bud around.

Dad seemed to accept that I
knew about such things.

Don't worry. She's safe with me.

Someone called for bowling shoes.
Adam and I eased down to the far lane.

Okay, little girl. Ready to party?

I was ready to take a big bite
of freedom before my time was up.

You gotta be sure.

Mom expected me home in ten
days. Of course, I was sure.

Let's hit the back room.

We ducked behind a stack
of crates, sat on the floor.

You really never tried this?

Like magic, a mirror and
razor blade appeared.

> *You're gonna love it. You'll see.*

I watched him pour powder,
yellowish white.

> *It will take you to heaven.*

Used the blade to chop the chunks
fine, draw two crooked lines.

> *Make you want to fly all night.*

He held the mirror to my face,
handed me a sawed-off straw,

> *Make you want to make love to me.*

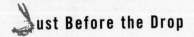ust Before the Drop

You know how you
stand and stand and stand
in line for the most
gigantic incredible roller
                                coaster
you've ever dared attempt.

Anticipation swelling,
minute by minute by minute,
you choose to wait even
longer, to ride in the front
                                car
and finally it's your turn.

They buckle you in, lock the
safety bar with a jolting *clunk!*
Hook engaged, the chain jerks
you forward. You start to
                                climb
crank-crank-crank.

Cresting the top, time
moves into overtime
as you wait for that scant
hesitation, just before you

                            drop

knowing you can't turn back.

You know how you feel
at that instant? Well, that's
exactly how it feels when you
shake hands with the

                            monster.

No Time Like That First Time

Fire!
Your nose ignites,
flameless kerosene
(and, some say, Drano)
laced with ephedrine

you want to cry

powdered demons bite
through cartilage and sinuses,
take dead aim at your
brain, jump inside

want to scream

troops of tapping feet
fall into rhythm,
marking time, right
between your eyes

get the urge to dance

louder, louder, ultra
gray-matter power,
shock waves of energy
mushroom inside your head

you want to let go
                                detonate,
                    annihilate barriers,
                    bring down the walls,
                unleashing floodwaters,
            freeing long-captive dreams
to ride the current
                            through
            arteries and capillaries,
                pulsing, rushing,
                raging torrents
            pounding against your heart
sweeping you away.

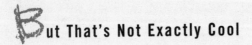

But That's Not Exactly Cool

So you sit and smile,
pretending like it's not
even fazing you,
not touching you at all.

So he looks you
in the eye, trying
to measure you,
find a hint of reaction.

And he says,
Tell me how you feel.

So you can't stand
it one more second,
and you close your eyes,
daring him to kiss you.

So he does, and it's
electric, high voltage,
stun-gun strength desire
jolting sinew and bone.

And he asks,
How 'bout another line?

If a Little's Good

More must be great, right?

Well, sometimes.
That time!

It didn't burn as bad,
nasal self-defense,
I guess.

And it launched me
to a place, very
near the gates
of heaven.

Adam took my hand,
led me the rest
of the way. No,
not quite all
the way.

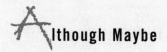# Although Maybe

it's a matter of semantics.
How does Webster define

        "all the way"?

Does it mean, start to finish,
an act of defilement,

        pure physicality,

no choice but yes, no
stopping now,

        no holds barred,

everything off, nothing
left to chance,

        all the way in?

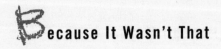ecause It Wasn't That

It was gentle persuasion.

I can't get enough of you.

Sweetest coercion.

My beautiful angel.

Magnet to metal.

I've got to have all of you.

It was hands, exploring
taboo places.

Oh, God! You're perfect!

Lips and tongue, not
far behind.

Let me eat you up.

Skin to skin, belly
to shoulder.

Sweet as puddin'.

It was body rush
after body rush,
intensity building.

Touch me there.

Hot flush, raging
blush, quick-start
ignition.

See how much I need you?

Ice flash, instant
crash, voices
outside the door.

No! Don't stop now!

Didn't Want to Stop Either

but one of those voices
belonged to my dad.

They were here just a while ago.

We scrambled to cover skin,
passion, and stash.

I didn't see them leave.

Trepidation, just this side
of anticipation, tingled.

They must be around somewhere.

The monster stomped up
and down my spine.

Kristina? Buddy? You here?

Adam looked at me and
whispered, "Who's Kristina?"

For Some Crazy Reason

I thought that was
the funniest thing
I'd ever heard.

Creepy, insane
laughter bubbled
up from my gut
like lava,
erupting
suddenly
in gigantic
heaving
gulps.

We were
busted.
I was
busted.

And I
didn't
give
a
damn.

Not Until the Door Opened

Guess who was there
with my dad.

Wha' the fuck you up to, Buddy?

Lince pounced through
the door, claws extended,
golden eyes growing black.

You two been messin' around?

Hair askew, buttons
undone, I thought it was
pretty obvious. But Adam
dared say no.

Well, what, then?

Damn, if she didn't
want to believe him.
I almost felt sorry
for her. The monster
shook me smarter.

Okay then. Fix me a line.

Like an Idiot

I took one too.
Things went from
weird to worse.

I mean, there I was,
snorting crank
with my dad,
my boyfriend,
and his other
girlfriend.

Something majorly
wrong with that picture.

The Monster Loves to Talk

He jumps into your head
and opens your mouth,
making it spout your
deepest
darkest
deceptions.
Making you say
all the things
you'd rather
not say,
at least not
in mixed company.

ad Said

I shouldn't be tootin'. My boss
almost caught me last time.
Think I could convince her to try a line?
I'd love to get her in bed.

Adam said,

Don't blame you there, man.
She's a babe, for someone
my mom's age. I'd do her too.
Think she'd go for a threesome?

Lince said,

Whoa, baby. Keep it in
in your pants, at least
till I take it out of them.
Anyway, three's a crowd.

I decided

Three is a throng.
Four's more.

I got up, headed
for the door, hoping
Adam would try
to stop me.
But lust is stronger
than love. And
monster lust
is unconquerable.

I Was Pissed

Anger seeped
from my pores,
vinegar sweat,
as I stomped
out the door,
into the night,
down the dark
sidewalk.

              I was hot.

Heart
jackhammering
in my chest,
pumping fever,
toenails to follicles,
blistering
veins and
brain cells.

              I was high.

I ran through
the alley,
inconsolable,
turned down
the sidewalk,
invincible,
five minutes
later,

I was scared.

Night Had Hung

a sultry, black curtain,
sequined gold.

It would have been
quite beautiful in another part of town.

But here, cars
cruised slowly,
checking out the
tightly knit groups
crowding sidewalks
and doorways.

Here, color
was everything,
skin color,
hair color,
the color of
your jacket.

Fair-skinned,
golden-haired,

I stood out like a moped
at a Harley rally.

I Thought I Knew the Way Home

but it all looked different,
covered in night,
and the buzzing
in my brain
put this sparkling
in my eyes.

It wasn't like psychedelic,
more like my eyes
were speeding too,
and didn't know
just where to focus
except on
points
of
light
in
the
dark.

Whatever,
I was
completely
disoriented.
And as I tried
to figure out
which way to go,
these three guys
in Raiders jackets
semicircled me.

*Hey, baby,
can we help you wit' som'thin'?*

Tried to Be Cool

Tried to sound tough,
asked if they could
spare a smoke.

> *Sure, baby.*
> *Anything you want.*

Took a cigarette, bummed
a light, and with a soft "thanks"
tried to amble away.

> *Hey. Where ya going?*
> *You ain't in a hurry, are ya?*

They weren't big, not football
players, but I was outnumbered
and felt it.

> *Yeah, what kind of*
> *thanks is that?*

The circle tightened,
moving me back, away
from the safety of the street.

> *Damn, you are*
> *a fine little piece.*

Think. Think! But my brain
moved too fast to process well.
My eyes gave it away.

> *Yo. I think this bitch*
> *been crankin'.*

That was license enough. Bodies
bumped, pushed me into
a doorway, blocked escape.

> *Ever done a three-fer?*
> *You gonna love it, baby.*

Hands

covered my mouth,
rough,
held my arms,
strong,
ripped my clothes,
vicious.

Fear danced
up my spine,
jolted
my brain,
dripped onto
the ground.

No! I
screamed
into dirty
flesh.
Not
this way!

Buttons burst,
zippers
opened,
I closed my
eyes, braced
for pain.

nd Then I Heard

a familiar voice.

Hey, dudes.
Whatcha doin'?

Adam took
command.

You not bothering
that little girl?

The trio
pulled back,
straightened up.

'Cause that just
isn't right.

Glared.
Stared.
Half issued
a challenge.

Nah, man. No need
to fight. Besides . . .

Adam pointed
to a black
and white,
two blocks
away and closing.

> You know what they do
> to rapists in prison?

Three Raiders Jackets

faded into the night,
dissolving like silver
and black nightmares.

Adam folded me gently
into his arms,
kissed my sobs,
stilled my quaking.

Don't cry, Bree. It's okay now.

The patrol car drew
even, slowed to
a crawl, window
rolled down, inquiring.

Remember, you're buzzed. Stay cool.

Glad he was there, scared
he was there, I dug deep
for a smile, waved
the cop away.

Come on. Let's go home.

Held Tight

to his shirt
all the way home,
clung fast like
a paranoid kitten.
Dad wasn't there,
no doubt bowling
off his own buzz,
so I asked Adam in.

We stayed up all
night, smoking,
talking, I struggle
to remember
exactly what
about.

Boys	*Chicks*
School	*Detention*
Art	*Sports*
Reno	*Albuquerque*
Mom	*Mom*
Dad	*Long-gone Dad*

Stepdads	*Boyfriends*
Gay sister	*O.D.'d brother*
Buddy	*Bree*
Adam	*Kristina*
Love	*Love*

awn Broke

A rose-colored rain
over distant hills.

We kissed for about
the thousandth time,

No promises,
no demands,

Just solid rebuilding
of shattered trust.

Then I said it.
He said it too.

I love you.
And everything
that went before

meant nothing.

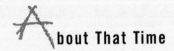bout That Time

Dad stumbled in,
looking like the monster
had boogied on off.

You still up?

Up, and flying high.
Was I supposed to go
to sleep?

Better get some sleep.

I walked Adam
to the door, promised
to see him later.

*You two didn't do anything
I wouldn't do. Did you?*

No way, Daddy dearest.
And where were you
when I needed you?

*'Cause a girl could get
into real trouble.*

Clueless

Dad went to bed.
I laid on the couch,
closed my eyes, let
the night slip into

        replay.

Exhilarating,
rocketing into my
mind, reaching
unimagined

        highs.

Depressing,
knowing when
I left, Adam would
stay. Would he

        downplay

spectacular
times together,
forget the best,
remember the

        lows?

As if I had
never entered his
life, never existed,
would he

                   toss

all promise of
tomorrow,
tumble headlong
into old

                 routines?

As if
he had never
told me
he loved me?

Was Supposed to Sleep?

Thoughts bulleted
in my brain, ricocheting,
creative side to practical side,
lustful half to hateful half.
Sleep? Yeah, right.

I got up, located cleanser
and sponge, scrubbed
the bathroom,
washed the dishes,
waxed the kitchen floor.

Wrote a four-page
letter to my sister,
told her I was in love.
With a boy.
I think I asked
for her forgiveness.

Wrote a poem, an epic, tinged
with dark humor,
decided to give it to my mom
because this was all her fault.
Somehow.

Went to the bathroom,
considered my growling stomach,
but the thought of food made me want to heave.
Settled for a beer. That went down fine,
so I had another.
And another.

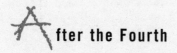

After the Fourth

No more writing paper,
nothing left to clean,
I turned on the TV,
thanked God for the
Jerry Springer marathon,
six great hours, filled
with pitiful people,
whose lives were way
worse than my own.
Hard to believe
the world is such
a screwed-up place.

I needed food, sleep,
but the monster denied
every bit of it.
Playing wasted couch
potato was all that I
could ask for.
And more.
Fading speed buzz,
escalating alcohol,
it was all I could
do to stay upright.
So I didn't.

Used Up

Burned out, adrift on a sea
of uncertain synapses,
a place where
your eyes
refuse to focus
and your brain
refuses to function.

Somewhere between
the transvestite
who slept with his
(her?)
mother's boyfriend
and the perky
blond
(transvestite?)
evening
weathergirl.

Everything
shut
down,
cerebral
ghost
town.
I
fell
into
sleep.
Deep,
dream-free
sleep.

Woke to Pounding

on the door,
insistent vibration,
building noise.

> *Bree? You there?*

Late-day sun
filtered through
cracks in
the blinds.

> *It's me. Open up.*

Late-day? How
long had
I slept? Only
hours?

> *I need to talk to you.*

Twenty hours,
as it turned
out. I tried to
open my eyes.

> *Please, Bree?*

Adam's tone
forced me into
the moment.
"Hang on."

Something happened.

My mouth tasted
like dead speed,
dying beer, and
foreboding.

There was an accident.

Coming

Jumped up, dashed
for mouthwash,
forgetting the
                    uncertainty
of legs, unused for
twenty hours, but
spurred to confront the
                              fear
in his voice, and
something more,
something too like
                    guilt.
Oh God, who was in
the mirror? Not Bree,
not Kristina, but some
                              evil
incarnation glaring
back at me, a horrid
red-eyed crone,
                    materialized

as if from darkest
dementia, nightmares
to come, hibernating

                inside of me.

Filled the Sink

with cold water,
dunked my whole head
under,
counted to ten,
came up,
repeated the process.

Came up again and
she had retreated,
still close,
I suspected,
but far enough
to let me
go to the door.

His Demon Showed in His Eyes

He stumbled in, tumbled
against me, clutching
like a scared little boy,
in need of his mama's grace.

She's hurt real bad.

Who?

Lince.

What?

Fell (or jumped) off the balcony.

When?

Yesterday.

Where?

Right outside.

I didn't
dare ask
       why.
Instead,
I let him
       cry.

He Told Me Why Anyway

She came home from the bowling alley,
went looking for me.
Found me.
Here, with you.

Heard us inside,
talking, laughing.
Looked in the window,
watched us kissing,
watched my hands,
running all up an' down you.

When your dad came home,
she waited for me to come outside.
Said she wanted to talk.
But she wanted more than that.
She wanted to erase you
from my heart.
Never could, Bree.
Never could.
And that's what
I told her.

The monster rose up hard then,
hard in her eyes,
She looked like an animal,
crazy mad,
diseased.
Spit in every word,
she swore
she'd get back
at you,
at me.

Next thing I knew,
she was on the sidewalk below,
still,
except for the blood running
red from her head.

They say it was an accident,
she tripped,
or leaned over too far.
Crankin', they said,
and she was.
Oh, yes, she was.

That's what I wanna believe.
Maybe someday I can.

But right now I think something different.

I never saw it coming.
Never thought she would.
I would have stopped her.

Could I have stopped her?

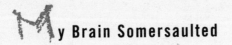y Brain Somersaulted

My heart picked up speed,
my stomach threatened
to 86 guilt,
drowning in bile.

> Oh, God. I'm sorry.
> *Hold me.*

I wrapped him tight,
hair dripping cool
around the stiffness
of his shoulders.

> Not your fault.
> *Whose, then?*

The answer, hanging
over my head like
a stubborn black cloud,
seemed obvious.

> Mine.
> *Don't say that.*

I pictured Guinivere,
golden-eyed wildcat,
crumpled against the
sad, cracked cement.

　　　　　　Whose then?
　　　　　　　　Plenty of blame to go around.

Too much truth in that.
And I never heard a thing,
dead to the world
for twenty hours.

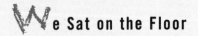e Sat on the Floor

Tangled up in each other,
a knot of emotions
desperate for release.

And the more we kissed,
the more we talked,
the more confused we became.

He loved me. He loved her.
He loved her first.
He loved me now.

I loved him. I hated her.
I hated him for loving her.
I loved him for loving her still.

He wanted me. He needed me.
He needed more to go to her, let her
know he loved her still.

I wanted him. I needed him.
I wanted him to forget her, needed
more to let him tell her he loved her.

When he asked me to go
along, some masochistic
piece of me agreed.

Fifteen Blocks on Foot and a Bus Ride Later

We walked through big revolving doors,
into the Land of Antiseptic.
My empty stomach rocked
at the alcohol/bleach perfume,
yet somewhere in that revolting scent
a lovely memory floated,
ghostlike.

The receptionist told us Lince was in ICU
and asked if we were relatives.
I'd seen enough soap operas to know
to nod an affirmative answer.
Adam played along.
I'm her brother and this is . . .
I held my breath
. . . my fiancé.

The lady didn't even blink behind her thick
gray lenses. She directed us to
the elevators. We got off
on the 7th floor. A nurse said
we'd missed visiting hours,
but since we were relatives
she'd let us poke in
through the door.

Intensive care is not a private place,
big windows allowed unobstructed
hallway-to-room views.
It was a sea of white.
Uniforms. Sheets. Curtains.
Floors and walls.
Why did that feel comforting?

ince Floated

in that white water world,
Guinivere upon the River Styx,
tubes intruding wrists and nose,
liquid-filled lifelines.

Adam let go of my hand and
I stopped in mute agreement.
This was his show.
I found the waiting room.

A dozen needs attacked me there.

> I needed
> food,
> fluid,
> soap,
> shampoo.

> I needed
> Adam,
> his heart,
> his promises
> his tomorrows.

I needed
to go home
'cause somewhere
deep down

I needed
my mommy.

And all that made me really
really need

a line.

Evening, When We Left

The breeze,
too hot
to cool
the blooming
flower of summer

                               night,

seemed to
ignite star
candles in a sky,
darkened as much
by mood as

                               time.

We found
the bus stop
in silence,
though I knew
he had something

                               to say.

Walked home
beneath
the celestial
cathedral. No kiss
at my door, only his

                              good-bye.

Not enough,
but how could
I beg for more? Did he
mean forever, or just for

                              now?

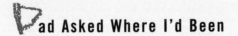ad Asked Where I'd Been

How's she doin'?

I opened my mouth
to tell him, realized
I didn't know. Adam
had given nothing away.

Heard it was touch-and-go for a while.

Still looked touch-and-go
to me, machines pumping
existence into her
through plastic tubes.

Too damn bad. Pretty girl.

Not so pretty now, Dad,
head to toe black-and-blue,
and shattered framework,
facing uncertain healing.

Hard to believe we just partied together.

He really didn't get it,
turned back to his TV. I
went to the refrigerator,
held my breath, looked inside.

Sorry, not much in there.

Moldy cheese, outdated
milk, peanut butter, and
soggy celery. I found an apple,
soft, but edible. Almost sweet.

We could go out to dinner.

My brain claimed I was
crazy to even consider such
a thing. But my insistent
stomach won the day.

McD's okay?

ne Hour

Tons of tasteless, useless, meaningless
food and conversation later,
two rounded, roiling
bellies pushed
back through
the front door.

Not that Dad didn't ask plenty of
questions, worthy of answers,
but how could I tell
the man who turned
his back on "daddy" status
how my life had changed?

How could I explain
gut-wrenching insights to
someone so lacking
vision?

How could I admit my
part in the current melodrama
to a psyche devoid
of guilt?

How could I share the
way my heart was breaking
when my confessor
didn't believe

in love?

Instead We Returned to Small Talk

which is probably all we'll ever manage,
all we'll ever get to,
if we get to anything at all.

We couldn't have spent more than
two hours, total, within three weeks,
tied up in trying to talk to each other.

Inter-family communication
must be an acquired skill.
He never even asked

if I'd gotten high before my little
Albuquerque adventure.
Never asked if I enjoyed

spending time with the monster.
He only wanted to know if Buddy
and I had done the dirty, perhaps right there

between his own disgusting sheets.
His question reeked
of voyeurism.

And he accepted my negative answer
with a smile that meant
he didn't believe a word.

I wondered if Mom
would have.

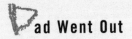ad Went Out

Left me

to
fret

to
stress

to
cry

to
choke
on
emotion
and

great
green
nose
clogging
gobs

in
sincere
need
of a
good
blow

instead,
I let
the
snot
drip.

Was Mid-Drip

when Adam knocked on the door.
I half considered pretending
I wasn't there.
Hurting.
Bursting.
Over him.
Over this whole sorry
pile of crap
I'd dug myself into.

But I wanted to see him
more than anything.
Needed to know
I hadn't imagined
the whole head over heels
thing. I had to go home
in a couple of days. I
wanted to go
still in love.

I found a paper towel,
let go a mighty blow
and went to
let him in,
even though I knew
I must have looked
very much like my
dead and buried grandma.

Okay, I Looked Awful

To anyone else,
he probably looked worse.
To me, he resembled an angel.
A poor, sad, beautiful angel.

His hurt swallowed mine,
like space swallows time,
and the two intertwine.
We tangled together
            I'm sorry.
Me too.
            I'm just so confused.
Ditto.
            I do know I love you.
Ditto
squared.

So of Course I Did a Really Stupid Thing

He pulled a bindle from his pocket,
tapped the sparkly powder inside.

Cooked up fresh yesterday.

Mother Kristina said no.
The monster stormed Bree's door.

That's my girl. Let's forget
the bullshit and fly.

We soared through the night,
well beyond daylight.

Funny thing about the monster.
The worse he treats you,
the more you love him.

I knew already that had to be true.
Blood geysered in my veins.
Thoughts stampeded across my
brain. Together, ecstasy.

You are the most incredible girl.
I never believed someone like you
would fall for someone like me.
But are you Kristina? Or Bree?

At the moment, all Bree.
"Kristina is who they made me.
Bree is who I choose to be. How
'bout you? Adam or Buddy?"

> With you, I am Adam.
> And you are my beautiful
> Eve. Let's run away,
> find our garden, live there
> together, happy. Naked.

dam

took me in his arms

    kisses melting

Unhurried hands lifted

    my shirt

Passion rose up in

    my heart.

hurt, forgotten ice

Pump. Pump. Pump

and a bit farther south

The monster-fueled

    inferno built

Adam's mouth moved

    lower, inch

I was ready to do it

    oh, so ready.

thigh to belly button

by trembling inch

right that very instant....

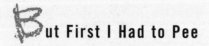ut First I Had to Pee

Passing the mirror,
I chanced a glance at Bree,
crank embers glowing behind
dilated black windows.
She didn't look half bad,
certainly not dead and buried.
In fact, she looked quite animated.

I dropped my jeans. And guess what
I discovered, already staining my panties?
That pesky monthly visitor
who shows, unbidden, on
your step, a true-blue party killer.

Only this time,
encouraged by the monster,
it blew across the threshold,
smashed down my door.
I staunched the flow, changed
my clothes, and went to tell Adam.

Flustered, flushed,
he swore he didn't care,
pouted and pleaded and cajoled.
But I was not about
to lose my virginity
in a fountain of
menstrual fluid.

How many times
have I regretted that decision?

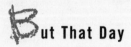ut That Day

there was still enough
Kristina left to feel

               humiliation,

still a smattering of
old-fashioned morals,

               somewhere

inside; still a healthy dose
of survival instinct, buried

               beneath

a childhood, fractured by
hormones, smashed by

               the monster's

fist and pressed into
memory by two-faced

               bravado.

So I Said

"No way."

        Why not?

"You know
why not."

        But you know you want to.

"I do.
But I
can't."

        Not right, Bree. Look what you've done to me.

And I
thought,
What did I do?

        You made me need you.

He brought
the crank.

        Made me have to have you.

He let
things get
out of hand.

        Not later. Not next time. Now.

And then
he took
my hand,

Put it right there.

showed me
how to make
things right.

Yes, just like that.

For him.
But what
about me?

# Girls Get Screwed

Not that kind of screwed,
what I mean is,
they're always
on the short
end of
things.

The way things work, how
guys feel great, but
make girls feel
cheap for doing
exactly what
they beg
for.

The way they get to play
you, all the while
claiming they
love you and
making you
believe it's
true.

The way it's okay to gift
their heart one day, a
backhand the next, to
move on to the apricot
when the peach
blushes and
bruises.

These things make me believe
God's a man, after all.

Considered That

As I considered my suitcase,
sitting empty and closed on the floor.

Empty and closed like Dad, not quite
hopeless, but not ready to be filled.

Empty and closed like Mom, writing a novel
to create the excitement lacking in her own little life.

Empty and closed like my sister, genetically
locked in a maelstrom of meaningless apologies.

Empty and closed like Lince, hovering in some
frozen netherworld neither sun nor rain could thaw.

Much too much to think about, I unzipped
my American Tourister and started to pack.

One Day and Counting

Mom called on her cell.

> *You ready to come home?*
> *Don't forget to get to the airport*
> *at least an hour early.*
> *Kristina? We've really missed you*
> *around here.*

Translation:

> You *are* coming home, aren't you?
> Your father's a dunce, so remind him.
> You *are* coming home, aren't you?

Dad called from work.

> *I took the dayshift so we could spend*
> *tonight together.*
> *Want to go out to dinner?*
> *Did you say good-bye to Buddy?*

Translation:

> We really should spend one evening together.
> The fridge is empty again.
> He's not over there boinking you, is he?

Adam called from the hospital.

> *Lince is off the respirator,*
> *but still in a coma.*
> *Can I see you this afternoon?*
> *I've got a surprise for you.*

Translation:

> Looks like she'll survive, with or without a brain.
> Are you still on your period?
> I'm on my way to pick up a bindle.

To Speed or Not to Speed?

I told Adam to come on over,
I wasn't going

        anywhere

then proceeded to fret,
as I did

        anytime

he and Lince popped up
together in a single thought,

        anyway

I had only this day to make
him remember me, however

        I could.

I knew it wasn't a great idea,
flying home, mostly high on

        the monster

or crashing fast, the
last tiny remnants of speed

        and I

fighting to feel good,
despite what the buzz

        had become—

low, that is, so low it
was hard to remember the

                                        best

of it. So of course I chose to
go for it. Adam, Bree, and
the monster were inextricable

                                    friends.

Couple of Toots

Skeletal lines, jaundice yellow,
evil little breezes up the nose.

One

inhale, awesome, mean, tiny
hammer blows to the brain, and I
didn't care who knew that

I was high,

(well, okay, I preferred clueless cops)
not Dad, who would be home
soon. He'd want one or

two

himself. Not the people next door,
who I'm pretty sure kept an ear
to the wall, waiting to see if

I would fly,

or attempt, like our wingless lynx,
to defy all instinct and natural
law, ball up courage, count to

three

and crest the edge in one mighty
leap. Or maybe she did just fall.
I wonder, as I wonder if

I,

         locked in a cage of dreamless sleep,
        a place where only the monster
            can drop you so hard,

heard the cry
   of a fallen
      broken
         bird.

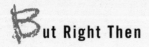ut Right Then

all I could think of, in
that speeded, heated moment,
was my own pain, stabbing
through the pleasure.

I asked Adam to hold me,
kiss me longer, harder.

Oh, God. I love you.

Begged him to help me
remember the taste of love.

How will I live without you?

Pleaded with him not to live
without me. Write. Call.

I will. I promise.

And I promised I would
come back to him.

I want to give you something.

I can't believe I let him,
me, la gallina extrema.

So you'll never forget me.

(The extreme chicken.)
Closed my eyes.

I'll always be a part of you.

Gritted my teeth, locked
into the love of the needle.

Right there, on your thigh.

And accepted Adam's tattoo,
the tiny heart a very big

Stashed under your skin.

symbol, forever bonding us,
his ink in my flesh.

It Throbbed   the Next Day

All the way home   red and raw, like
  my eyes, drained   of tears, denied
    sleep's healing,   staring at the
      glare of midday sun in
       vibrant blue sky at
        20,000 feet.

Red and raw like   my belly, not even
  McDonald's to   soothe its empty
    demand ('cause   Dad, of course,
      cranked it up when he got
       home—so much for
        dinner out).

Red and raw like   my heart, pried
  from Adam's, the   two beating, no
    longer together,   but a thousand
      miles between them when
       only yesterday they
        thumped in
         unison.

Red and raw like   my brain, unable
to shut down,   thoughts crashing
like electrons   orbiting a nucleus
of dueling emotions. Wanting
to stay high. Knowing I
should want to come
down and stay
that way.

Still Wasn't Down

When We Landed

High-rise casinos,
each with a "got
rich" story or two
and thousands of
sad little secrets,
gigantic glittering
towers of glass
and ungodly neon
intruding upon the
beauty of the July
dusk, yet waving
a welcome home,
midst a bayou of cement, asphalt shingles, tinted panes, fake wood
siding, and lingering in the distance, an ocean of sage-embroidered
playa, vast as time itself, those very seconds, hours, eons locked
within the fringe of great crustal blocks most call mountains.

Kristina had seen it all before.

Kristina was home.

Bree saw it all through new eyes.

Bree was a stranger.

Tightened Airport Security

No one greeted me
on the far side of the jetway,
no relatives, no friends,
only slot machines.

Tugging those two
carry-ons, upper thigh
itching like crazy beneath
a tight pair of jeans.

I wandered toward
the escalators, a 50-foot-long
mural of blue Lake Tahoe
flanking me on my left.

8-foot-tall showgirls
in purple boas (and not
much else) smiling
at me from the right.

Kristina drawn left,
Bree to the right,
the monster started to
retreat just in time.

I Saw Them

before they saw me—
the whole fam-damily turned out to greet me:

Jake, sweaty and animated,
auburn hair   (And where did *that* come from, Mother?)
ruffled, freckled face   (Thank God I missed that recessive gene!)
handsome
with summer color.

Leigh, on summer break,
too "Brittney-ish"   (So much of Mom's platinum beauty!)
to really be gay,   (What a waste—like a butch would care!)
legs to die for,
unshaved in short shorts.

Scott, face losing
stress as he   (Hard day, or another argument?)
put work behind him,   (Mom could have done worse—and had!)
tall, lean, and great
looking for 40.

Mom, somehow prettier
with laugh lines,   (Would I be able to say the same?)
visible from here,   (Would I ever even be that beautiful?)
and a smile that could
light a starless night.

Right at that minute,
she saw me.   (And, just for an instant,
                            her smile was all mine!)

Then She Caught Sight

of something
>
> not quite right,

something
>
> not quite familiar.

She hesitated,
>
> unsure

that I was me.
>
> Her smile

dissolved,
>
> ghostlike.

But then
>
> she waved,

and my family
>
> flooded me.

Homecomings Are Strange

You come home,
    and everyone talks
      at once
    and everyone asks
      questions,
            but no one waits for the answers.

Instead they talk about themselves,
    what they've been
      up to,
    what they're going
      to do next,
            as if you're a photo on the wall.

And then they talk to one another,
    forgetting you've just
      flown in,
    forgetting you're in
      the backseat,
            forgetting they've already said it all.

And you want to shout,
  can't you see
    I'm here?
  can't you see I'm
    brand new?
        Can't you see me at all?

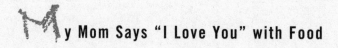

My Mom Says "I Love You" with Food

So we went out to dinner. Not McDonald's, either.
We went to a buffet. A mega casino-style buffet:

Salads—Oriental chicken; wilted spinach; ambrosia; three-bean;
crab (at least that's what they call it); potato (three kinds); pasta
(five kinds); carrot & raisin (nasty); and, of course, green.

Entrees—pizza, lasagna, mushroom ravioli; fried chicken,
roasted chicken, chicken piccata; mahi, halibut, and deep-fried
cod; mashed, baked, scalloped potatoes; vegetables; and on the
carving board, roast beef, roast turkey, and roast loin of pork.

Desserts—apple, cherry, and lemon meringue pies; angel, carrot,
and triple-chocolate cakes; pastries, cookies, rum balls, and
truffles; cobblers and bread pudding; soft-serve ice cream, with
all the fixings; and for sweet-tooths on a diet, strawberries
(forget the diet, top with whipped cream!).

So Mom gets two plates (low carbs), strawberries (no whipped cream).
Leigh gets three, eats half of each, skips dessert.
Scott eats most of three, with a brownie and ice cream for dessert.
Jake finishes four, down to the gravy; tops that off with three desserts.

As for me, still battling
the monster
for brain and
stomach space,
I picked at a
single plate.

Home Sweet Home

Our pretty
little place on a
hilltop acre, native
sandstone and imported
compost, Mom's handcrafted
oasis in a northern Nevada high
altitude valley, not really a valley, but
more a depression in the eastern Sierra
foothills, where mountain streams fed snowmelt
into a shallow, silver lake, and everything managed
to stay green, despite high desert heat and wild winter winds,

looked like it welcomed me	looked like it threatened me
looked just the same to me	looked completely different
and I was happy to be home	and I was undeniably sad
and I never wanted to leave	and I wanted to turn and run
wanted to call my old friends	wanted to call my newest friend
wanted to confide everything	wanted to keep it all to myself
needed to boast about the best	needed to confess the worst
needed to hold up	needed to break down
had to remember	had to forget
had to find Kristina.	had to hide Bree.

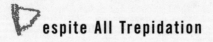espite All Trepidation

Despite the monster,
fluttering in and out of my head
like some demented moth, drawn
to whatever light might be left there,

    despite Bree,
    demanding I find a way to get high,
    as if I had a clue where to get crank
    back here in Kristina Land,

    despite Leigh,
    helping me lug one suitcase,
    her hand annoyingly pinching mine
    with every tug, every pull,

        despite Jake,
        dropping the other suitcase
        down an entire flight of stairs,
        spilling shampoo, lotion, and tampons,

despite Scott,
smelling depressingly clean,
while my own speed-induced
body odor reeked ever stronger,

    despite my mom,
    insisting I looked fabulous, having
    dropped four or five pounds, all the
    while wondering if anorexia had arisen. . . .

REGARDLESS

My   spotless

mauve room   with pretty pink

butterflies on one   windowed wall

and a big old bed   worthy of dreams

invited me   into the familiar

offered to rest   my weary body

and soothe my   sorrowful heart.

🗡 Slithered Down the Hall

into the haven
of the bathroom,

        shed

my clothes,
showered,
scrubbed my

        skin

until I thought
it might blister,
studied my thigh,

        found

likely signs
of infection.
Bree shrugged,

        Kristina

silently screamed
at the angry
green pocket of pus

        beneath

the purple welt—
Adam's forever
symbol of love.

The Door Opened

I did scream then.
But it was only Leigh.

> Hey, it's only me.
> Kinda jumpy, aren't you?

"Did you need something?
I'm naked you know."

> I've seen you naked before.
> 'Course I've never seen that before.

She pointed to the tattoo.
What could I do but ask her opinion?

> In my opinion, you've got one nasty
> infection. Did you sterilize the needle?

Thinking back, I wasn't so sure.
But I said, "Of course he did."

> He *did*, huh? Your hard-bodied,
> dark-haired dream boy did this?

So then I had to tell her everything.
Except I left out about the monster.

> Well, I hope that's the only infection
> he gave you, in love or no.

So then I got my back up. Played
defense to her quarterback sneak.

> *No need to get your back up.*
> *I was just kidding, and of course*
> *girls can carry STDs too.*

So then Bree felt much better, while
Kristina felt really bad.

> *I know you're sorry. No worries.*
> *Let's chalk it up to jet lag.*

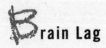rain Lag

described it better,
synapses quieting, gray
matter shutting down, except
the pain center part, Leigh's elementary
nursing—alcohol, hydrogen peroxide, and a
dab of Neosporin—had only managed to make
the aching mess hurt even more, although
she probably killed off a germ or two.

At least, lost in the center
of my bed, I didn't have to wear
jeans or jammies or even panties.
Naked, in that cool tangle of cotton
sheets, I felt myself slip far, far away,
deep beneath an indigo ocean. Down, down,
into a silent, lightless land, and there, in the darkness
I found my Adam.

Funny thing, your brain,
how it always functions on one
level or another. How, even stuck in
some sort of subconscious limbo, it works
your lungs, your muscle twitches, your heart;
in fact, in symphony with your heart, allowing it
to feel love. Pain. Jealousy. Guilt. I wonder if it's the
same for people, lost in comas. Is there really such a thing

as brain death?

Silence

          shook me awake.
          I groped into
consciousness
          room dark,
          blinds closed,
shadows
          undulating in
          air-conditioned
waves.
          Midday,
          I thought, house
emptied
          of people,
          of pets,
of life,
          Nobody home.
          Just me for
company,
          no one
          demanding

conversation

                or explanations.
                I was

alone,

                and I liked
                it that

way.

On the Nightstand

I found a prescription bottle
and three notes.

The first was from Leigh:

> *Had some antibiotics I forgot to finish.*
> *You won't get a whole treatment, but*
> *they haven't expired. Not the way you're*
> *supposed to do it, but couldn't hurt!*

The second was from Mom:

> *Your father called to make sure you made*
> *it home okay. You are okay, aren't you?*
> *I told him everything was fine.*
> *It is fine, isn't it?*

The third was from Jake:

> *Some guy named Adam called. At least I*
> *think his name was Adam. He also said*
> *Buddy? First he asked for Bree, then*
> *changed it to Kristina. Who's Bree?*

Good question.

Went Straight for the Phone

dialed Adam's number, forgetting
the area code was different.
Got some
creep's cell
phone by mistake, and asked
for the man of my dreams.

Don't think I know him, but if
you talk real dirty,
I can fake it.

Bree giggled. Kristina wanted
to puke, thanked him anyway,
tried again.
Head dizzy,
hands shaky, 505 area code
inserted correctly, I got his mom.

Buddy's at the hospital. Lince
opened her eyes today.
I'll tell him you called.

Kristina felt relief. Bree felt rage
and a burning desire for a couple
of lines. I
thought
about the one time I actually sat
down and talked to Adam's mom.

Tough thing for two boys
when their daddy
turns his back on 'em.

Turned his back, packed a bag
and hit the highway. Left
his family,
broke, in a
lousy two-bedroom walk-up.
Never said "bye," let alone "sorry."

Sorry speed freak. Least I got
to wear my face minus bruises
and swollen eyes.

Finally without tears, until
her oldest son died, shootin'
speedballs—
just enough
meth to stay wide awake for
the heroin wild ride over the brink.

Michael took after his dad.
Never too much, never enough
of goin' right out of his head.

What did that make Adam?
Watching his dad choose
the monster,
seeing his
brother lie down for the demon,
how could he want to party too?

Buddy's all I've got left. I pray
to the good Lord he makes
better decisions.

And, knowing all these things,
perhaps more intimately
than I ought
to, what did
that make me?
I thought about praying too.

Changed

my
mind.
No
doubt
the
good
If You do still care, Lord, please keep me safe.
had
weightier
things
to
worry
about
than
the
half-
hearted
apology
of
a
crashing
crankster.

The Phone, Still in My Hand, Rang

I jumped, like a bee had just
given me a nasty hello.
I returned the favor

with a totally foul, "Yessss?"
(Then thought,
jeez, what if it's Adam?)

Hey, Kristina. It's Sarah.
How are you? How was your
trip? Tell me all about it!
How was your dad? Sweet?
Did you meet any cute boys?

Sarah—my best friend since
4th grade. Crazy smart,
pretty in an Irish sort of way,

with embarrassing freckles
and wicked red hair she was
forever trying to tame.

Was it hot down there?
It's been miserable here!
Did your dad have a pool?
Did you get a tan?
What did you do for fun?

What could I tell her?
How much did I dare?
That is, if she ever gave

me a chance to talk.
How much did she
really want to know?

Did you do any shopping? I
already got school clothes.
What did you do for the 4th
of July? We went
up to Virginia City.

What day was today? The 10th!
Dad never said a word
about fireworks.

The 4th of July had slipped
on past, with me held
fast in the grip of the monster.

We're going camping.
Want to come? My mom
said it's okay. I hate to spend
a whole week, alone
with my parents and little sister.

I told her I'd ask and call later.
My brain needed a rest—not
to mention my left ear.

Kristina could listen
to Sarah talk for hours.
Bree was ready to scream.

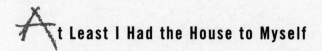

At Least I Had the House to Myself

I downed an ampicillin,
splashed peroxide on my

            wounded

thigh, which actually
looked a little better, the

            heart

more pink than violet,
the pain more a soft

            pulsing

reminding me with
a steady beat of an

            emptiness

so complete I had
no clue how to fill it,

            loneliness

so heavy I had
no idea how to lift it,

            need

so intense I had only
one way to relieve it:

            a bitter drink

of its very source—
the deep well

             of the monster.

Considered

the Reno crank scene,
or what I knew of it.
Legit entertainment—

music,
magic,
comedy clubs.

Legal and semilegit—

gaming,
sports betting,
light night carousing.

Legal, semi-immoral—

adult revues (aka "titty shows")
gay clubs, strip clubs, swap clubs,
beyond-the-city-limits prostitution.

Such activities,

24-7,

practically invited

the monster's

participation.
Remote desert
dwellings, travel
trailers and

                              sad, little
shacks, went up
in flames regularly,

                              victims
of ether-fed fire.
Oh, yes, there was
crank in Reno,

                              waiting
for me, calling
out to Bree.
All that was left was

                              to find it.

Suddenly, However

all those days with little
or no sustenance hit me in one awful instant.

Lucky me! Mom's kitchen
was a whole lot better stocked than Dad's.
(Not to mention a whole lot cleaner—
no mega-cockroaches allowed!)

Summer fruit.
Garden veggies.
Leftover roast beef.
Homemade bread.
Hand-churned ice cream.

I'd almost forgotten how great a cook
Mom was, at least when she wasn't
too busy writing or going through one
of her "I'm not your damn servant!" phases.

Double lucky me.
It seemed she was going through one of her
Suzy Homemaker stages.

Fresh salsa.
Homemade chips.
Leftover chili.
Cherry pie.

I felt like I'd died and
gone to God's grocery store
in the sky!

My Luck Ran Out

'Cause after	I
finished pigging out,	I
really wanted	
a cigarette.	
Nicotine's a	
strange addiction.	I
didn't even realize	I
was hooked until	I
couldn't have one.	No
one at my house	
smoked, at least	not
so you'd notice.	Not
my mom. Smoking	
causes wrinkles.	Not
Scott, who had	
a family history	
of emphysema.	Not

Leigh, who said
they made
your hair smell
like an ash
tray (only true
if you don't
smoke). Surely   not
Jake, the
ministud athlete.   Nope
                                  I

was most definitely
out of luck.
For the moment
anyway.

It Got Worse

because just about then,
my mom came home.

> Good. You're up. You looked dead
> to the world, so we let you sleep.

Leigh shadowed her
through the door.

> "Feeling better? We went shopping.
> I needed a new swimsuit in the worst way."

Mom put an armful of bags
on the counter, ignoring
my crumbs.

> I got you one too. Your old one
> is pretty ratty.

Leigh reached into
a Macy's bag, extracted
it for approval.

> "Cute, huh? She wanted to get you a tank. I
> insisted on a bikini. You *do* still like pink?"

Mom looked at the hot pink
crochet, as if for the first time,
shook her head and clucked,
> *Better try it on. Can't show too much*
> *skin at Scott's company picnic.*

Leigh glanced down
at my T-shirt hem,
barely covering our
sisterly secret.
> "Nope, wouldn't do. Wouldn't
> do at all."

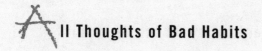ll Thoughts of Bad Habits

vanished within a deluge of normalcy.
 Scott's company picnic was an annual

   family affair, fifty computer specialists,
     plus kids, wives, significant others, et al,
        eating, drinking, and being otherwise merry

     on the water slides, wave and wading pools
       at a decidedly fun place called Wild Waters.
         Beyond all things wet, there were go-carts,

        minigolf, an "invest your entire allowance
          here" arcade, and amusement-park-style rides.
           The day began early, ended late, and we always

           had a blast. So why didn't it sound inviting? I
             was home. Everything was the same, everything
               exactly as it should be. Everything, that is, except

                                           me.

Went to Try On the Swimsuit

Few things are quite as

          humbling

as cinching yourself up
in a completely

          revealing

bikini and standing
in front of a full-length

          reflection,

rotating like a bird on
a spit, trying to admire the

          naked truth

staring back at you:
body slim but not

          fine-tuned

boyish hips, just
barely qualifying as

          curves,

uncertain breasts,
cup size

          stalled

somewhere between
A (plus) and B (minus),

          womanhood

desperately trying
to escape,

                  succeeding
once a month,
like it or not,

                  ready or not.
(At least that wasn't
currently a problem!)

The Tattoo, However, Was

It did look better,
but it still didn't look good—
a bright pink, semi-heart-shaped thing,
blue ink hiding somewhere beneath my skin,
not an easy thing to hide in an itsy bitsy bikini.

Band-aids were problematic. A little
one wouldn't cover it, but one of those big
square dudes would draw everyone's attention,
guaranteed. Besides, have you ever seen a Band-aid,
floating in a swimming pool? Would you want to
be responsible for such a disgusting thing?

And even if one did manage to stay
on midst gushing gallons of chlorinated
water, what would all that wet
wildness do to the just forming
scab and retreating infection?

Still, I couldn't beg off.
Wild Waters Day was important
to Scott's "leg up the management ladder."
It was Mom's day to strut her stuff in
her own itsy bitsy bikini.
And it was always a summer hit for us kids.

If I said I didn't want to go,
Mom would check for a fever for certain.
Even if she didn't find one, it
would open the door for questions
I really was in no mood to answer.

Questions I knew I'd have to answer soon.

As I Pondered

my problem, the telephone rang.
Jake happily informed me—not to
mention everyone else—it was
Adam/Buddy on the far end of the line.

"Hello?"   *Hey, Gorgeous. I miss you.*

      Melted butter.

"Oh, Adam. Me too."   *I can't stay on long. Phone
                                            bills, you know.*

      Hot butter burned.

"Okay."   *Just want you to know
                                            I love you.*

      Burned good.

"Me too. Always."   *Lince is coming home
                                            tomorrow. She'll be okay.*

      Burned bad.

"I'm glad."   *Bree? I've been thinking.
                                            We're a long way apart . . .*

      Sizzled.

"I know."   *So I think we should give
                                            each other permission
                                            to see other people.*

      Spattered.

"You want
my permission?"

        Welted.

"I don't need your
permission, Buddy.
And you obviously
don't need mine."

        Scarred.

*You have mine. Just think
of me from time to time.*

*Well, okay then. Better go.
Keep in touch.
I really do love you.*

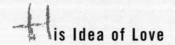is Idea of Love

sure didn't mesh with mine.

"I love you, let's see other people."
Interesting
sentence structure.

"Lince's coming home.
Let's see other people."
Unusual
paragraph construction.

My face flushed
tears poked my eyes,
scar tissue twisted my heart,
wrapped itself around arteries,
closed tight around my jugular.
I coughed pain.

I never went to Albuquerque
expecting to find love.
I thought it had found me there,
followed me home.

I never came home,
expecting to lose
love in the space
of one brief
telephone call.

Is it always so short-lived?

Mom Knocked on My Door

I found that strange.
She never knocked.
                    May I come in?
Never asked for permission
to come in. Permission.
That word again.
                    We haven't had a chance to talk
                    since you got home.
Then she looked at my face,
all puffy and pissed, read
everything she needed to there.
                    Looks like we've got a lot to talk about.
                    But maybe this isn't the best time?
I wanted to talk. Needed to.
But how could I possibly talk
to her? She was mom.
                    I know I'm your mom and not always
                    easy to talk to. But I'm here for you.
I was ready for a lecture.
Why did she have to choose
that moment to try "nice"?

> *I want to hear all about your trip. Let*
> *me know when you're ready.*

Big girls don't cry, especially
not in front of their mommies.
But a cloudburst threatened.

> *I hope you're hungry. I'm making*
> *your favorite—lasagna and garlic bread.*

I was hungry (somehow).
I was tired (still). I was hurting (inside and out).
And more than ever, I wanted to walk with the monster.

Over Lasagna and Garlic Bread

I talked about airplanes.
        I talked about lonely seatmates,
third-run movies, and pretzels
        (for this price!) in place of meals.

I talked about Albuquerque, bowling alley
        etiquette, Los Alamos–grown cockroaches,
and walk-ups in decidedly bad neighborhoods
        (omitting the part about my own little nighttime foray).

With some prodding, I talked about Dad,
        his job, and (lack of) girlfriends;
I talked about his philosophy, somehow sadly yet
        to ripen into something resembling maturity.

With a lot more prodding,
        I talked about Adam aka Buddy
(omitting everything of use to anyone
        interested in blackmail).

Considering his recent treachery,
                   it was easy enough not to gush
about his hot bod, wildcat eyes,
                   incredibly perfect lips, and intuitive hands.

And, mostly because everyone knew
                   it anyway, I talked about how, despite
his undying love, he had given us both
                   permission to date other people.

Leigh Knew

there was a
whole lot

           more

to the story,
of course.
But I'd never
told her

           secrets,

and trusted
completely
she would
never betray

           mine.

Still, just in
case, I
never dared
mention

           sex,

interrupted
by periods;
Lince,
interrupted by

           drugs;

or my own
infatuation with
the monster's
spectacular

rock and roll.

No, these
secrets
belonged strictly
in my own
private closet.

Later

Leigh climbed into my bed,
moved very close to me,
her proximity strangely
unsettling.

> *Want to talk? I do.*
> *I miss how we used to talk.*

I recalled a time, not so long
ago, when snuggling with
my big sister was
comforting.

> *Tell me more about Adam. Is he*
> *really your very first boyfriend?*

So why did it bother me now,
when I so needed
the consolation
of touch?

> *I'll tell you about Heather. She's*
> *not my first, but she tops the list.*

Heather? Lesbians had names like
Bobbi or Jo, didn't they?
"Heather" belonged to a
model or cheerleader.

> *She's a cheerleader. Well, a song*
> *leader, and pretty much perfect.*

Leigh was almost perfect herself.
If she were taller, *she* could be
a model. Picture-perfect
lesbians. I had to laugh.

> *What are you laughing about? Didn't*
> *know cheerleaders were my type?*

Didn't know cheerleaders could *be*
that type. Which got me thinking.
What else might those peppy
cheerleaders do?

Tucked That Away

and tried to focus on my   sister

going on and on about being in   love

with a girl:

       their meeting,   touching

       accidentally,   connecting

       immediately,   interwoven

       hand in hand,   heart-to-heart.

And even though I loved my   sister

had accepted her   eccentricities

I found it hard

to listen to	detailed
descriptions,	abstract
ambitions,	relevant
observations,	hers and mine.

Wild Waters Day Dawned

hot, crystal blue—perfect for watery fun.
   I donned my new bikini, disguised
      the tattoo beneath a hot pink   While
         gauze cover-up, and on   waiting in line,
            some lunatic whim   we ran into Trent,
            called Sarah to   another longtime friend,
            come along.   who on his 16th birthday made
                       the huge mistake of climbing out
                       of the closet and waving a big hello.

Of course, I was good with it. We
   were best buds, no matter what,
      and, of course, there was   Since he
         the Leigh factor. But   outed, Trent
            others in our school   had been teased,
            were not quite so   humiliated, beaten, even
            open-minded.   semitortured by some pickup
                       truck cowboys who didn't have a
                       clue about the real meaning of masculinity.

So there I was at Wild Waters, trying
to look extremely cool at the
coolest place in town,
with chatty Sarah
Baker and Trent
"the gay guy"
Rosselli.

Turned into an interesting day.

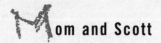om and Scott

wandered over to the group
picnic area to join the company
brownnosers and nibble.

Leigh and Jake went off together,
racing to see who could reach
the top of Black Widow first.

Trent hit the wave pool.
Sarah hit the bathroom—she always
showered before entering the pool.

I opted for an inner-tube float along
the Lazy River, mostly because of this
very cute lifeguard, perched overhead.

And there was Bree, smiling seductively,
and I swear that poster boy lifeguard
smiled right back.

And in that righteous moment, complete
clarity. Bree was not an invention,
not a stranger.

Bree was the essence of me.

Whether That's Good or Bad

I can't say. I just know it's true.

Bree opens doors

Kristina wouldn't dare
knock on,

like that cute lifeguard's—
not to mention Adam's,
even if that one had recently
slammed in her face.

But Bree insists on having
things all her way.

So when Trent and Sarah
came trucking up,
bickering and tittering
and doing all those little
cutesy friend-type things,
Kristina never minded.

Bree wanted to tell them
to shut the hell up, go
away. Let her play.

For a while,
without the monster
whispering sweet
and terrible
nothings,
Kristina was still in charge.

But Bree was watching.

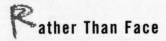ather Than Face

total embarrassment, I
told Trent and Sarah I'd
meet them at Black Widow.

> They looked at me,
> looked at what I was looking at,
> hard-bodied and tan on his tall tower.

> Trent gave me a thumbs-up.
> Sarah broke out in giggles.
> Then they graciously provided space.

I invited Bree to take over while
Kristina took cover. She bent forward
from the waist, shook her dripping hair,

> straightened, flipped it backward,
> and without a single thought to the
> puffy pink heart on her thigh

(let alone its artist), she marched right
over to that lifeguard tower, looked up
and, without drooling at all, asked,

"Do you get a lunch break?"

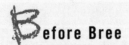efore Bree

that would never have happened.
Whatever she'd done to me,
for me, and basically

           in spite of me,

she'd given me a whole
new sense of self.
I never knew

           I could play the vamp,

do it so well, flirt
with total aplomb,
and not only that, but

           look good doing it.

Before Bree I never
knew such sheer, depraved
forwardness could

           be so much fun.

So I went with it,
jumped right into the role
of shameless flirt.

           Girls responded

with pointed whispers,
haughty laughter and, as
I myself have often done,

    with evil eyes.

Bree, of course, couldn't
care less. In fact she thrived
on any and all attention.

    Guys responded

to that with solid
once-overs, come-on smiles, and
in Brendan the lifeguard's case,

    with phone numbers.

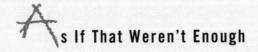

As If That Weren't Enough

I sprinted off in search of my friends
and (literally) bumped into Chase
Wagner, Reno High's storied bad boy.
Kristina would have offered a quick
apology and scurried away.

It's not like Chase was in
the running for Mr. America.
He looked like a linebacker,
one who didn't play much
in the sun—the freckles on his
cranberry skin almost pulsed pain.

But Bree found his bedroom
eyes—glacier blue—and brooding
demeanor quite the turn on.
"Hey, Chase," she cooed.

He scoped me out like an old
tomcat, ogling a brand-new canary.
Do I know you?

Kristina knew enough about *him*
to think she ought to flee.
Chase Wagner could be
hazardous to a person's health.

> *You look familiar, but not, so maybe*
> *I'm thinking of someone else.*
> *What's your name?*

Just like that, she had him.
If she wanted him. Her game was no
less dangerous than his. "Call me Bree."

Right Then, Three People

shouted, "Kristina!"
Time to beat a face-saving retreat, so
I smiled and told Chase I'd catch him later.

> I looked around and saw Mom,
> waving to come and eat,
>
> Leigh, minus Jake,
> gesturing to come share a towel,
>
> Sarah, at the top of Black Widow,
> watching Trent's wet ride down.
>
> "Not hungry yet," I shouted to Mom.
> To Leigh, "Be there in a few."

Then I joined my oldest, bestest
friends in the world, tried to think
of something to talk about
besides lifeguards, bad boys,

and this person named Bree,
growing stronger inside me,
convincing me to be someone
I never dreamed I'd want to be.

I know you should be able
to share such news with best friends,
but I felt pretty sure they'd never
relate and maybe refuse to forgive

      me for trading in the tried-and-true
      for a test drive of the dark side.

Still, When Brendan Came By

I left my friends with my sister, took
a walk to the back of the park, the eyes
in back of my head noting envious stares.

> Brendan noticed, too.
> *You related to those people?*

"Pretty much." I bummed a cigarette,
inhaled like it was the healthiest
thing a person could do.

> *The pretty one looks like you,*
> *but the others don't.*

My turn for a jealous jolt. But I had a secret
weapon. "The pretty one is my lesbian
sister. The others are my cousins."

> *Lesbian! Really? I never met*
> *one before. How about you?*

I laughed. "Of course I've met one, if my
sister is one. Oh, you mean do I lean that
direction? No way. I prefer male hardware."

> *I like what you've got, too, li'l*
> *sister. At least, what I can see.*

Male hardware? Must have read it in *Cosmo.*
Whatever. Brendan touched my hair, made
a move like he just might kiss me. . . .

*Damn. There's my boss. Back
to work. Call me, okay?*

I wondered if I could. I'd always waited
for boys to call me. Which is why I never
talked to any except Trent. And Adam.

*By the way, beautiful, what's
your name? In case you call.*

Twice in one day! I almost told him
the truth but realized the fantasy was better
and rested completely in Bree's hands.

Went Home

tired, tanned, and
stuffed on barbecue,

Scott insisted

high on life,
nicotine, and
purloined booze,

Chase invited

elated, pumped
up, full of Bree's
magical ego,

Brendan inflated

chastised, brought
back down
a notch or two,

Leigh instigated

then all the way,
chest-deep into
shit when

Mom finally noticed

the tattoo, my
meaningless, forever
symbol of love. Still,

Bree swore

whatever
punishment
lay ahead,
only one thing
could have
improved
that phat,
fabulous day:

a big bite
of the monster.

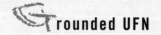

Grounded UFN

> *Until further notice. No*
> *excursions, no calls.*

How unfair could you get?
Couldn't she just decide how mad to be,
then mold the consequences to fit?

> *I'm so disappointed in you!*

What else was new? She was only good
with "all I could be" when it involved
a straight-A report card.

> *Don't you realize this could*
> *scar you forever?*

Well, duh, Mom. It already had,
though not in the way you imagined.
Couldn't you have asked about that?

> *Why can't you be more*
> *like your sister?*

Did she mean look more like her? Be
PhD bound? Or maybe she wanted me
gay? Lesbians and pregnancy rarely mix.

> *How can I trust you to make*
> *good decisions?*

Oh, great. Here it came. No driver's
training, no driver's license. Their
way of keeping me cooped up forever.

> Driver's training is on hold.
> And to keep you from feeling
> cooped up, you can pull weeds.

Fine. I was almost 17, would never
drive, and now I'd spend my summer
yanking goats' heads.

The Problem with Being Grounded

is it gives you a whole lot of
unavoidable time to

think.

Not even pulling weeds can
take away your ability to

plot

all the varied and wonderful
things you might do to

get even,

or at least to make up
just a smidgen

for time lost

to TV and yard work
and house cleaning.

Time better spent

camping with old friends
(even slightly annoying ones),

partying

with great-looking new friends,
and expending a few brain cells

with the monster.

She Cut Me Loose

Two weeks before
Back-to-School,
gave me her credit
card and a ride to
the mall, her way of
apologizing without
saying she was sorry
for trashing my summer.

Jake wanted to come
along, but I told him
I'd crawl into bed
and stay there rather
than haul my little
brother around the
mall. He went fishing
with Scott instead.

Didn't matter much.
Summer had dissolved.
New clothes and a few
new tunes just might
improve my "sour
outlook," as she so
lovingly termed it.

I usually despise trying
on clothes but, finally
free, I meant to make it
an all-day affair, shop
every store, including
Victoria's Secret. Guess
who I ran into there?

The Reno High Varsity
Cheerleaders, all buying
new undies and bras to
shape those tight tanks
and sweaters (football
weather in Reno is an
exceptionally mixed bag).

Those goody-goody girls,
flipping perfect cartwheels
and pert little ponytails,
most definitely accelerated
their metabolisms. The only
question was: how?

I waved to Trent's sister,
Robyn, then pretended
to browse, watching them
yak a hundred words a
minute, and I knew my
suspicions were accurate.

Pondered That

while I picked out
my own underwear.
As I handed the saleslady
Mom's credit card, someone
tapped my shoulder.

*Hey, Bree. Can I see
your panties?*

Chase! I tried to think
of a witty comeback,
managing mostly to look
like a stuttering fool.
"Uh-oh, uh—old or new?"

*Either, or. Better yet, both.
What's up? Where you been?*

Like he'd been looking
for me since Wild Waters.
Like I'd been avoiding him.

*You haven't been avoiding me,
have you?*

Why would I? What
he might lack in looks,
he more than made up for
in fringe benefits.
I explained about the tattoo.

You really wanna piss her off,
try a piercing. Want to see mine?

I couldn't find studs in his
ears, lips, or tongue. Which
pretty much left one place.
"Didn't it hurt?"

Like a mother. But it feels
awesome now.

He guided my hand
just south of his zipper.
Kristina recoiled.
Bree—well,
Bree was Bree,
to Chase's great pleasure.

Hee hee. So want to take
a little ride? Got my truck outside.

I started to protest.
I had some serious
shopping ahead.
And Bree or no Bree,
I wasn't about to do
Chase Wagner.

*No strings. I just want to get
to know you better.*

Where had I heard
a similar tale?
I was about to give him
a definite no when he
sweetened the offer.

*I've got a little toot, if you're
so inclined.*

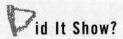id It Show?

I mean I'd

        thought

                about

                        the monster

        dreamed

                about

                        the monster

        lusted

                for

                        the monster

        regretted

                knowing

                        the monster

        but I hadn't

                touched

                        the monster

in over a month.
Hadn't even seen it.

Thought I might be over it.
Was it still alive in me?

Could it still have such
a solid hold on me?

We Drove Down by the River

parked beneath towering cottonwoods.
Strange, how intensely desire
builds when the monster waits
at the far end of a drive.

On the way I learned, for a bad boy
Chase was incredibly smart. Webster
would envy his vocabulary, he was up on
current events, could quote Keats:

> *Give me women, wine, and snuff*
> *Until I cry out hold, enough!*
> *You may do so sans objection*
> *Till the day of resurrection; for*
> *Bless my beard they aye shall be*
> *My beloved Trinity.*

No mirrors, no blades, Chase reached
deep inside a pocket, withdrew an
amber bottle with a tiny spoon attached
to the lid. He set it on his knee.

> *Hey, you're shaking. You're not*
> *scared, are you? We don't have*
> *to do this, do anything at all. We*
> *can just sit and talk if you want.*

"I'm not afraid, Chase." Not of him.
Not with him. In fact, I felt quite safe.
It was monster desire that made me
tremble. Chase noticed.

> Take it easy with this stuff, Bree.
> It brings even good people to their
> knees. Don't get me wrong. I
> like it, too. Just keep cool.

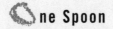ne Spoon

I was cool.
Two, I was too
cool. Three,
sub-Arctic. Four,
my mouth hit
monster mode.
Chase could barely
keep up. We talked
     about:

Good girls	*Bad boys*
Smothering moms	*Indifferent moms*
Disappointing fathers	*Obnoxious fathers*
Stepfathers—one	*Stepfathers—three*
Annoying little brothers	*Brothers with very big footsteps*
Summer trips	*Boring summers at home*
Junior years	*Senior years*
Early graduation	*College boards*
Cheerleaders	*Football players*
Artists	*Poets*
Tattoos	*Piercings*
Ex-boyfriends	*Ex-girlfriends*
Dreams	*Doubts*

Punishments	*Loneliness*
Old friends	*New friends*
Gay friends	*Lost friends*
Desire	*Addiction*
The monster	*More monster*
Kristina	*Bree*

Had to Explain

about Bree/me;
by then, he had
already asked to

                    kiss

me, and I let him
because I really
wanted him to,
and it wasn't my

                    first kiss

nothing like
that one, in fact,
maybe it wasn't
even my

                    best kiss

but it was pretty
fine, and the fact
that he had asked
will forever make

                    that kiss

stand out in my
mind, touch my
heart, make me
remember a

                              kiss so tender

it made me cry.
He held me then,
smoothed my hair
and I asked him to

                              kiss me again

and he did, over
and over, until
I thought we might
melt together,

                              fused by kisses.

In That Quite Hot Moment

a park ranger cruised by,
took a good, long look.

Maybe we'd better go.

"I should get back anyway.
My mom will wonder if I don't
spend enough of her money."

Ha, ha. I can always help.

As we drove away, he pulled me
close, rested his hand on my knee,
shifted between my legs.

Can I see you again?

"Any time, Chase." Any time.
How weird was that? A few months
back I would have said no way.

Soon?

As soon as I could break away from
Mom's watchful eye. Chase sure
wasn't her type. Was he really mine?

I like you, Kristina.

"I like you, too." I did. He
was nothing like I had imagined.
He was bright, intuitive.

Or do I like Bree?

Even if he did ask hard questions.
Jetting on the monster in spectacular
fashion, I didn't know how to answer.

> *Doesn't matter. What's in a name?*
> *That which we call a rose by any*
> *other word would smell as sweet.*

Chase Wagner and Bill Shakespeare.
Talk about your strange bedfellows.
I was in line for that ménage à trois.

Chase Wanted to Walk Around the Mall

with me, but I knew I wouldn't get much
shopping done if I went on a kissing
spree. A word of advice:

Never shop on crank.
Your brain moves beyond the
speed of light as you wander through
a familiar store. First, you can't find Juniors.

Once you finally do, you need the restroom first,
then you get all turned around again.
Then, you can barely take it
all in. Sizes. Styles.

Colors. Trends.
Everything looks great on
those goofy mannequins, so it's got to look
better on you, right? You grab an armful, stumble to a

dressing room, try on all those darling clothes
and nothing you like fits. So you leave silk
and velour and suede behind, settle
for two identical pairs of jeans.

Then you hustle off to the
next store and repeat the process,
only this time you leave with a couple of
tees exactly like a couple you bought last year.

And when you realize that, you laugh your
butt off, but really don't want to hassle
with returns or exchanges so you
decide to accessorize instead.

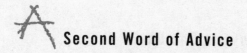 **Second Word of Advice**

If shopping for clothes on crank
is dumb, trolling for jewelry,
belts, and shoes is something
just this side of insane.
Suspenders?
Don't think so.
Nikes. Vans. Doc Martins.
One of each?
Maybe next time.
Scrunchies. Barrettes. Berets.
Ebb the sable flow?
Uh-uh.

I was stressing
over earrings when
another hand touched
my shoulder.

I thought you were going to call.

Brendan.

Two Guys in One Day?

Almost too much to consider,
although Bree found the prospect
quite intriguing. So then I had
to explain GUFN again.
"Today is the first day
she cut me loose."

                    Sounds like a reason to party.

That was funny. But it was time
to catch my ride home. Since Brendan
was my mom's type—tall, handsome,
and gainfully employed—I let him walk
me out. Mom was parked right in front.

                    Is she always so punctual?

I laughed like he was the wittiest
man alive, and promised to call,
wondering what was up. With me.
Had I lost one boyfriend, to gain
two? And how could I possibly
want *these* two, opposite
squares on the chessboard?

                         Damn, your mom is fine.
That wasn't funny at all. I had to
live with my mom, obey her rules,
accept her punishments. But I would
never accept her as competition.

                         Not as fine as you, of course.
Okay. Better.

Mom Wanted to Hear All About Brendan

I told her what I knew,
hoping I didn't talk too
much. Or too fast.

He's really cute.

Oh, great. Mutual attraction.
I almost opened my mouth,
thought better of it.

Did he ask you out?

In a manner of speaking,
I supposed. Out. In. I
doubted he was picky.

Do we need to have the talk?

At that, I really had to
stifle Bree. Let me tell
you, it wasn't easy.

He did seem like a nice boy.

Seeming and being are
two different things. You
seem nice, too, Mommy dearest.

Anyway, did you find some clothes?

I showed her what I
bought, and she grinned
a killer smile.

At least you're consistent.

I had to laugh, speeding
along with the monster.
Consistent? Not!

Inconsistent Me

could barely look at dinner.
I told Mom I ate at the mall.

                    What?

What, what?

                    What exactly did you eat?

Quick, Kristina, think.
"Stir-fry. You know,
fast food Chinese."

                    Did you eat all your veggies?

OMG! Here I was, busting
my brain on first-class speed,
and all she cared about was if
I'd consumed my greens?

                    'Cause you can't stay smart
                    eating only junk food.

Stay smart? First I had
to get smart, and it
wasn't about to happen
holding hands with
the monster.

                    Besides, vegetables give a girl
                    a healthy glow.

Damn. Wasn't I glowing?
Then again, even if I was,
it could hardly qualify
as healthy. Still, Mom
didn't insist I share the
dinner table.

It's only leftovers, anyway.
By the way, a letter came
for you today.

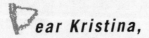

Dear Kristina,

Hope everything's okay. Hope you're okay.
Things are okay here.

My mom got a new job and she's dating her boss.
He already thinks he's my stepdad or something.
Says I'd better think about what I want to do with my life.
Besides party, that is.
I hate him already. You know?

Lince is home and I guess she's better.
She has to go to PT—physical therapy—every day.
She's learning to walk and talk, just like a baby.
It's weird, really weird.
I try to spend time with her, but it's hard. You know?

I'm sorry about that phone call.
I didn't mean to upset you.
I was at the end of a three-day binge.
Too long without food and sleep.
Your brain starts to play tricks. You know?

I do love you, Kristina.
You were a summer gift, one I'll always treasure.
You were a dream I never wanted to wake up from.
You opened my eyes to things I'll never really see.
You're the best thing that will ever happen to me.

Be safe. Be smart. Stay you.

Adam

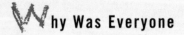hy Was Everyone

suddenly worried
about my IQ?
I sank into my

down

pillow-top,
reread every word
twenty times, right

down

to his signature.
Adam had a poet's soul.
I put the letter

down

and considered crying,
wondering how loving
him could bring me

so far down,

wondering how to stop
loving him, wondering
if the monster would soon

let me come down.

Did Cry Then

Climb-and-dive on the crank coaster,
I unlocked my heart, let the hurt out.
And then, like he was listening
at the keyhole, Chase called.
(He even asked for Kristina.)

> *Hey, sweetheart. Just checkin'*
> *up on ya. You okay?*

Let's see. Speedin'. Wantin' tobacco.
Cryin' over a guy I thought I was over.
Probably going to start my period—just
in time to encourage a few new zits right
before school started. "Fine."

> *Really? You don't sound fine.*
> *Can I make you feel better?*

I told you he was intuitive. Even
if he wasn't the type I could
bring home to Mother. Yes,
I liked Chase Wagner.

> *I'd sing to you but I'm pretty*
> *sure that wouldn't help.*

I jumped into his well of ever-present
cheerfulness, gulped deeply,
laughed out loud. We talked until
Scott needed to use the phone.

> *You probably won't sleep*
> *much tonight. Think of me*
> *once or twice?*

At least. I hung up, feeling much less
alone. Pulled out my journal and
started to write. Wrote all night.
The monster and I had a lot to say.

Chase Was Right

I didn't sleep much that
night
and not for the next
day
or three afterward,
either.
Sarah invited me
over,
I told her I felt
under
the weather,
both
to escape inevitable
questions
demanding uneasy
answers
and to consider my
options:

possibility number

one,

Chase, likely;

two,

Brendan, maybe;

three,

someone altogether new.

Who knew?

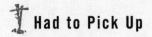# Had to Pick Up

my student I.D. card so I bummed a ride
from Chase, told Mom I was going with Sarah.

It was the first time in a long time I'd out and out
lied and it bothered me. For about five minutes.

I walked down to the 7-Eleven to wait for Chase,
anticipation rumbling in my empty gullet.

The sight of his red Toyota pickup brought
a smile to my lips—and more, inside.

We shared a seat, we shared a smoke,
we shared a kiss or several.

At school, Chase waited with me in some long
lines. Yearbook. Class schedule. Student body card.

I even smiled for the camera. I had to, with Chase
checking out my student body, grinning like a toad.

Back in the truck, more kisses and a cigarette of my
own (pilfered from his pack, pilfered from his mom).

He dropped me off around the corner from my house,
gave me a stick of gum and a big, wet good-bye kiss.

It might have been the perfect day except just
as I closed the door, Scott happened to drive by.

I learned a valuable lesson about lie construction
and Mom gave me plenty of time to consider
how to do it better.

UFN Again

I

        sat on my bed, absentmindedly
        tracing the lopsided
        heart-shaped scar,

didn't

        read, didn't write. All I did
        was think about my personal
        evolution. Where did I

belong

        with my relative innocence
        gone? Where did I fit?
        I felt like I had fallen in

to

        a critical state of limbo.
        With my old friends mired
        in status quo, how could I explain

my

        summer enlightenment? My new
        crowd—if three guys and Guinivere
        qualified—was not what my

mom

(or I) expected. I wondered if I should
confess that her sweet, intelligent
little Kristina did not exist

anymore.

eigh Headed Back to School

Mom drove her to the airport.
I waited until they hustled off, late,
then asked to stay home, claiming, "Cramps."

Mom gave me a look, but I could prove
the cramps were real. Leigh gave me a big,
tense hug, made me promise to behave myself.

The minute the car turned the corner,
I was on the telephone, completely
misbehaving.   "Come over, Chase."   *Now?*
                      "Right now."   *Where's your mom?*
                      "Just hurry."

Need arose like an angry red dawn.
I paced until the dogs warned
a stranger had just arrived.

                                        How much time
                                        do we have?
                      "Not enough."   *What do you*
                                        want?
                      "Everything."   *Will I get you in*
                                        trouble?

          "Probably."
I didn't care. I needed to feel
good. We snorted, we smoked.
I asked for,   "More."   *Don't think you*
                                                  should.
          "Please!"   *Take it easy,*
                                                  Kristina.
          "Can't."   *Your mom will be*
                                                  home soon.
          "I know.
          That's why
          I can't."

Chase Left Me with Goodies

He didn't want to, told me

no way,

but Bree, mistress of persuasion,
knew a trick or two

to get her way.

Kristina swore to keep her in
check and she tried, but

no way

to slow the electric impulse flow,
our brain began to plot. How

to get away

from the confines of GUFN?
Sweet-talk Mom?

Little chance

of that working, a crazy
idea soon hatched

to sneak away

for one spectacular last
summer fling.

Insanity,

that's what it was, school
starting in only two days.

Watched the Window

as I picked up the phone and dialed.
Bree cooed a throaty hello.

Hey. I'd just about given up on you.

I could not admit to GUFN. Not
again. I concocted
some lame excuse.

No problem. Want to get together?

I did. Chase or no Chase, I wanted
to see what Brendan was made of.
Bricks, mortar, flesh, bones.

I'll pick you up. Where and when?

Let's see. Wait for everyone
to hit the hay, extra half hour,
scale down the wall . . .

That's pretty late.

Very late. But I'd definitely be
awake. I coughed up the fact
I was sneaking out.

Okay by me. Just don't get caught.

No duh. I didn't plan on
getting caught. Still, what could
they do if I did? Ground me forever?

What sort of party would you like?

Damn, direct. Not even sure
if he indulged, I said I'd bring
the toot if he'd bring the beer.

Sounds like a deal I can live with.

Mom's SUV turned up
the driveway. Deal sealed,
I said good-bye.

See you tonight, luscious.

Luscious? Plain old white
bread me? I liked it. At least
I thought I did then.

Hid Out in My Room Until Dinner

made sure to gag down   every scrap of spinach,
          so both my mom   and my mouth
                    would keep quiet.

I still had a valid cramp   excuse so I packed it
          in early. Uh-huh.   Sat in the dark, lit
                    as the starry sky.

Listened to the sounds   of my normality: familiar
          footsteps in the hall;   whispers; laughter; baying
                    at the moonlight.

And it occurred to me   for one uneasy moment
          that every move I had   made lately might have
                    started a landslide.

What if I couldn't go back?   What if I died in the crash?

Almost immediately,   the monster soothed
          me, confused me   with a deeper question.
                    What if the ride was worth it?

I mean, who wants to   trudge through life, doing
   everything just right?   Taking no chances means
                 wasting your dreams.

  How can I explain the   pure chilling rush of
   waiting to do something   so basically not right?
             No fear. No guilt.

  How can I explain   purposely setting foot on
    a path so blatantly   treacherous? Was the
             fun in the fall?

Hoped Not

As I softly opened my second-floor window,
peered down at the cement walk below, took a   deep breath.

Fingers clutching the upper sill, toes stretching
for the first-floor trim, I managed to   touch down

safely. It may have been the safest moment
of the night, in fact. Gulped   into darkness,

I let my eyes adjust, felt the breeze lift
goosebumps, listened for signs of household   disturbance.

No motion. No sudden snitch of a light switch.
No sound but distant coyote song, I   silenced

my conscience, quieted my screaming nerves
and slipped away unnoticed,   for the moment.

No streetlights, no headlights, the world
seemed to sleep beneath my feet as   I ran,

a mustang over moonlit playa; a cheetah
in high gear. No fear, no brakes,   consumed

by some irrational itch to cruise along
shadowy thoroughfares, traveled   by demons.

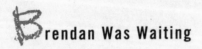

Brendan Was Waiting

in a battered mud-colored Bronco.

Climb in. You look great.

Winded. Hair plastered by my
escape sprint. He was a liar.
A smooth, gorgeous liar.

Wanna go up to Chamberlain Flat?

Secluded five miles up a rutted
dirt track, the played-out mine
was a notorious party spot.

Supposed to be a party up there.

Anything could happen at a party
up there. Good things. Bad things.
Truly evil things.

Ever hear about Evan Malone?

Evan Malone, urban legend—eighteen
and in league with Satan, skinning
goats up at Chamberlain Flat.

My brother went out with his sister.

So he was more than just a parental
fabrication meant to scare kids
away from abandoned mine shafts?

He was real, okay. Kyle met him.

Met him and what? Dressed up like
Halloween, prayed to the devil,
and sacrificed hoofed animals?

Shared a bong. Said he was creepy.
Major understatement, if the dude
was really for real! If pot made you
buddy up with Satan, you could keep it!

But don't worry. Evan's long gone.
I reached for a whiff of courage.

Far fuckin' out! Beer's in back.

We Bumped up the Road

Doing 40 or so   spilling some
          foam of   summer-warmed brew

          and busting our   guts, laughing.
I watched Brendan's   muscular hands

try to shift,   missing gears,
          try to steer   around potholes,

          not quite evading   most of them.
I studied his face,   mentally tracing

bone structure   a model would kill for,
          high cheekbones   perfect white teeth

          all sheathed in   Mediterranean-
flavored skin,   iced mocha,

begging to be   sipped, so I did.
          I swear, every   guy you kiss is

          so different.   Each has a unique
essence, each a   significant style.

Brendan was eau de   lavender, vanilla,
            Heineken, Crest   and top-notch speed.

            His style was   *"No is not an acceptable
answer."* He was   Bree, with a penis.

Saturday Night

          postmidnight, 30-some hours till
          back to the books, the party had

hit high

          gear. Pot smoke hung, a skunky
          green curtain, but I didn't want to

fall low

          so I indulged in another big snort
          before inhaling a couple of tiny tokes,

mostly

          to satisfy the incredible urge to pollute
          my lungs. I topped that off with a Marlboro,

landing

          on just about the perfect plane, just about the
          place I wanted to be. Not too speedy, not even close to

straight

          falling into the yo-yo rhythm of crank, pot,
          beer, tobacco, the sensational motion and emotion,

up and down,

          Brendan hanging tight, though I suspected
          he might desert me, take off on a flirting binge. And,

oh, god,

                the jealous stares of girls I had envied
                not long before, girls suddenly, strangely on fire to
know me,
                though they had never once in the past returned
                my smile. And now, instead of Kristina, they got to
know Bree.

Brendan Stoked the Fire

Let's take a walk.
I was game to play the game. We wandered
   off, found a soft sitting
spot in a patch of crispy brown wild wheat.
         Come here, Bree.
As he pulled me onto his lap, I wondered if
   I should confess my double identity.
Instead, I let him kiss me. Hard. Hot.
         Oh, man. I'm hot.
He shed his shirt and the moon revealed
   perfect, tanned muscles. He started
to unbutton mine, silencing my protest.
         Shhh. Don't say no.
"I can't. I mean, I never . . ." Crank-enhanced
   goosebumps lifted as he moved
his hands gently across my skin. "Stop."
         You know you want to.
"I do, Brendan, I really do. But I can't.
   It's the wrong time of the month."
I'd decked him. He slapped back.
         Then, why did you call?

I let Bree answer. "Not to get laid, incredible
    as you are. Is that all you think I'm
about? What if I told you I'm a virgin?"

                                    I'd call you a liar.
Bree wanted to joust, but Kristina thought
    about a long walk home and put Bree
back into her box. I looked him in the eye. "No lie."

Paydirt!

The "v" thing. Is it   every guy's dream
to take something   so tenuous and make
it totally, solidly his?   But Brendan softened
immediately, offered   to forgive me if only I
promised to let him   be first. I wasn't sure
what I needed forgiveness for but I said
okay, then proceeded to thank
him as only Bree—and the
monster—could.

air Mussed

clothes cockeyed,
makeup smeared,
I would have looked
fairly suspicious if I
had walked through
the door that night.

But I didn't have
to and never once
pondered getting
caught as I stood
tiptoe on the first-
floor window trim,
stretching to catch
the ledge and crawl
back inside my window.

House dark, no sound
but Jake's snoring
through the wall, I
laid in bed, watching
a ghost dance on the
ceiling, nose sucking

up sweat, tobacco, and
eau de Brendan,
wondering what Adam
was up to until the sun
poked through the curtains,
less than an hour later.

High

For two days, too much crank,
                      no sleep, liquid diet. The first

day of school was a nightmare.
                      Good thing I wasn't a freshman.

I'd have gotten lost, somewhere
                      between gym and the chem lab.

(Almost did, in fact.) I collected
                      handouts; tried to follow list upon

list of curricular expectations;
                      tried, failing miserably, to conquer

new locker combinations; avoided
                      eye contact with teachers, staff, and

most definitely school police;
                      ducked Sarah and Trent so I didn't

have to listen to their chitchat;
                      spent lunch far from anything close

to food, even though I trembled

from near starvation. All the while

feeling like my head would burst

from thinking so damn much when

all my brain wanted to do was

close down and fall deep into REM

sleep. I considered climbing under

the bleachers, letting it do just that

before I did something really dumb

like passing out, but just about then

the final bell rang.

ay One

blessedly behind me,
I rode the belching bus

                                        home

wondering how I would
possibly make it to

                                        school

the next day. Craved down
time when I had to gear up,

                                        sustenance

though I might throw it up,
silence when I knew my

                                        family

would be waiting to share
news of the day. The very

                                        monotony

I had lately disdained
cried out to me: *I am*

                                        essential

without me you will
wither, like this

                                        summer

folding up into fall;
freeze hard, water in

                                        winter
awaiting the first breath of
spring; uproot, grass in a

                                        wind
blown into tornado;
parch, like earth denied

                                        rain.

Mom's Car Wasn't in the Driveway

I thanked my, for once,
       lucky stars, went
          inside, ignoring
             Jake completely.
                Scoped out the
                   fridge, grabbed
                      a handful of red
                         grapes so sweet
                            you could never
                               even fantasize them.

Downed them like
   candy, went back
      for more, chased
         them with fudge
            swirl Häagan-Dazs.
               No homework, I
                  went into my
                     room, fell straight
                        into bed and the
                           sleep of the dead.

Mom must have
    thought me dead,
        when she found
            me hours later,
                tried desperately
                    to shake me from
                        the devil's deep slumber
                            embrace, shouted for
                                Jake to bring icewater,
                                    threw it in my face.

Which Roused Me

riled me,
made me
        want to
        scream.
Instead
I made
        a major—in
        retrospect,
not the best—
decision.
        I creaked
        to sitting,
thought
twice,
        but when
        she insisted
I drag my
rubbery
        bones to the
        dinner table,

I looked
her in the
eye and for
the first time
in my life,
told my
mother,
"Fuck you."

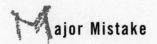ajor Mistake

Her eyes popped wide, her jaw
dropped like concrete. She reached
out and shook me.

> *What did you say?*

Even caught up in confusion,
I knew better than to repeat myself.
I shook my head.

> *Tell me again.*

Okay, she was testing me.
I flunked completely.
"I said, fuck you."

> *That's what I thought you said.*

Mom's turn for firsts.
She slapped me so hard my teeth
rattled and snot flew.

> *Don't ever say that to me again.*

I dissolved into exhausted
tears, wondering why I'd done it.
Mom broke down too.

> *Kristina, what's going on with you?*

I couldn't tell her the truth.
What kind of lie might do? I started
with a genuine, "I'm sorry."

Oh, God, I'm sorry too.

She sat down beside me
on the bed, put her arms around
me, hugged tight.

You're not in trouble, are you?

Trouble? All sorts of trouble, oh,
yes. But not the kind she was worried
about. "No, Mom."

These new friends . . . are they . . . okay?

Why couldn't she just say
what she meant, ask if they'd led
me down the path to hell.

You've got so much promise. . . .

Then again, if she did, would I
own up? Confess that I had taken
the lead on this perilous journey?

Please don't throw it all away.

My mind churned love. Mom loved
me. Adam loved me. I suspected
Chase might love me,

     I love you, Kristina Georgia.

(I was pretty sure Brendan
only loved the big "v.")
Who loved me more?
Who loved me most?

     Now, please come down to dinner.

Did

I sat at the table,
brain blank, head

spinning,

something
that sounded
suspiciously liquidy

whooshing

between my ears,
trying not to look
like the space cadet
I felt like,

struggling

to form coherent
sentences around
megabites of chicken
and corn bread,

waiting for

the ax to clobber
me. But Mom never
said a word about the

reason

for the red marks
across my cheek, and

                                not

only didn't punish
me, but let me off
GUFN.

                                Forgiveness

granted, I made some
decisions: appreciate
family, focus on
school and hunt

                                for Kristina.

Mostly Managed That

for the next week.
Hit a reasonable
educational stride,
settled into the rhythm
of classrooms, quizzes,
study halls, homework.

Hung out with
Sarah and Trent,
swapped summer
vacation stories
(majorly editing mine),
tried out for honor choir
and actually made it, despite
a voice gone raspy from excess
and mushrooming allergies.

Did my best to absorb
the energy of family,
meals, Sunday church,
and a Labor Day camp out.
And I managed all that,
barely thinking

about the monster
or wondering what
Chase or Brendan or Adam
might be up to.

Until in one fateful day
Adam wrote, Brendan called,
and Chase showed up to drive
me home after school.

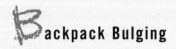ackpack Bulging

I climbed into Chase's truck,
slid close. "Where ya been?"

>   *We moved to Sparks. I had to transfer.*

Solid explanation. Still,
"Why didn't you call?"

>   *I did. You were grounded. Remember?*

That excuse was shakier.
"Not for the last two weeks."

>   *I wanted to give you some space.*

Pregnant pause, giving
himself some space.

>   *Kristina, I know I'm not exactly your type.*

I looked him in the eye.
"I don't think I have a 'type.'"

>   *I thought it might be the lifeguard type.*

Reno wasn't the "biggest
little city." It was a
small-town gossip mill.

>   *Not that we have an exclusive thing, I know.*

My cheeks burned. "No, we
don't. But I really like you."

>   *I needed to hear that. I like you, too. A lot.*

"I went out with Brendan
because I was flattered."
I dared to confess, "I never
had a boyfriend until
last summer."

That's hard to believe, Kristina.

Taking that totally wrong,
I huffed, "Why?
Because I'm such a slut?"

No. Because you're so beautiful.
Tell me about last summer.

By the time I finished, I still
loved Adam. But I was falling for Chase.

So Why

       was I so hot to return
the phone message, waiting
       for me to come home?

Brendan:

       Give me a call. I want
to see you again. This time
       I'll bring the refreshments.

"Refreshments?"

       I'd perched on my
pedestal for a whole week.
       How fast could I make it down?

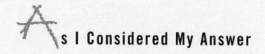

As I Considered My Answer

I noticed Adam's letter, sitting on the counter.

Dear Kristina,

How's school? I hope I can make it through this year.
It's really tough, what with worrying about Mom,
Ralph (can you believe she'd like a guy named Ralph?),
and Lince. She's talking better now, and can get
herself to the bathroom. I guess that's good.

I saw your dad the other day. It was kind of strange
because he never even mentioned you. Of course, he
was with a new woman. (Not bad, considering she's
with your dad. Ha, ha.) Maybe he doesn't want her
to think he's old enough to have a daughter your age.

Are you going out with anyone special? Half of me
hopes so. The other half wants you to always be
mine. There's a pretty cute girl at school, Giselle, giving
me the eye. She looks a little like you, in fact.
I think I might ask her out.

333

Maybe you didn't want to hear that. But you're my
very best friend, the only one in the whole world
I could tell that to. I want to hear everything
about you, too. Kind of weird, huh?

So do you have a boyfriend? Is he a jock or what?
(Wink, wink.) How safe are these letters, anyway?
Does your mom read them? I wonder if Giselle
parties. Doesn't everyone? Okay, maybe not.

Write soon. Love, Adam

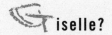iselle?

He liked some girl named Giselle?
Did she speak French (or just give it)?

Maybe I didn't want to hear that?
Why did I read his letter anyway?

And what was up with Dad?
Why hadn't he called?

Was he a Daddy Judas?
Had he sold me out?

Should I call Brendan?
Set myself up?

Would I truly let him be first?
Was I ready to lose the big v?

Should I call Chase instead?
Ask him to score for me?

Would he do it if I asked?
Walk a slender wire for me?

Did I want to risk honor-roll status?
Chance further alienating my mom?

Had I lost my mind completely?
Did I really want to get high?

You Bet I Did

The monster
        shouted, *Where have you been, my*
                sweet Bree? Hurry back to me.
        My blood pressure bloomed, my head
pounded.
        Need rose up, pumping violently
                through my veins. All I could
        think of, as I reached for the phone
on my
        nightstand, were fat ivory lines,
                waiting to whisk me to a
        netherworld, far beyond my
door.
        Chase was "busy" Friday night. So I
                did a really intelligent thing.
        Called Brendan for a date and
asked
        him to make a buy. "Can you get me an
                eight ball?" I figured an eighth
        of an ounce would last awhile. It cost
me

$250, which I was saving to buy my
       first car. But hey, I probably
wouldn't have my license

for

years. Illicit fun settled upon, I put on
       my most innocent face and went
to gift my family with half-hearted

company.

Could Hardly Wait for Friday

Though the voice of my virginity nagged,
the lure of the monster was stronger.
Besides, I could always say "no."
Couldn't I?

Pretending to be the perfect gentleman,
Brendan arrived at my door,
introduced himself politely.

We told my mom and Scott we were
going to dinner and a drive-in double feature.
But food and movies were the last
things on our minds.

Not that we necessarily had the same
things on our minds. As we drove up the
mountain, his hand crept up my leg.

I let it do exactly that as I watched for a safe
spot to pull over. We drove back off the highway,
deep into a grove of fresh-scented evergreens.
Carried a blanket back into the trees.

He pulled out a bindle, which looked a bit short,
and a six-pack of beer. For the next twenty minutes,
we snorted and drank, climbing to a very tall buzz.

We talked and joked and giggled.
And it all seemed just like it should.

Until it didn't anymore.

It Started with a Kiss

Crank-revved, pistons firing full bore,
passion firecrackered in tiny bursts
from thigh to belly button.

Oh, baby,
I want you so bad!

"B-b-bad to the bone?" We laughed,
but it wasn't a joke. Not for long.
My shirt tore open. "Wait."

I've waited for weeks.
Put up and shut up.

Kisses segued to bites. Bruises.
Pain rippled through my body.
"Brendan, please stop."

No. You promised,
you damn little tease.

Off came my shorts. Down went
his zipper. I realized I was in
serious trouble. "I'll scream."

Go ahead. No one can hear
but skunks and coyotes.

Still, as I opened my mouth, his
hand slapped down over it. Those
sublime muscles hardened.

Just relax.
You'll love it.

My brand-new Victoria's Secrets
shredded, and I felt the worst of
Brendan pause, savoring my terror.

They all love it.

Had he done it a different way, I
might have responded with excitement.
Instead, I froze as he pushed inside.

There it is.
Oh, God. There it goes.

It went, all right, with an audible
tear. Pain mushroomed into agony
and all I could do was go stiff.

You weren't lying,
you bitch!

I laid there, sobbing, as he worked
and sweated over me. Stoked by the
monster, it took him a long time to finish.

Give me a line,
I'll give you an encore.

He pulled away, sticky and bloody.
Throbbing inside and out, I didn't move,
didn't dare look him in the eye.

What the hell
is the matter, Bree?

I stared up at the clouds, gathering
into gloom, shrouding the moon.
"My name is Kristina."

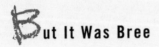ut It Was Bree

who got me on my feet

helped me to the car

put me on the seat

kept me semiupright

on the long ride home

Bree, who staunched the blood

straightened up my clothes

unsmeared the makeup

brushed my hair smooth

willed strength against the aching

claiming body and soul

Bree, who understood

that, wasted on crank, there

was nothing I could do

but plot future revenge.

Not a Blink of Remorse

Brendan didn't say a word
most of the way home. He
drove slowly, just under the
limit. I watched him, out
of the corner of my eye.

He didn't look so perfect
anymore. His nose had a
bump and his eyebrows
almost joined. And, of course,
I knew what he was made of.

Finally, he found a few words—
his thank you for the gift he had
stolen, the one I should have given
and never could again. I will
remember them forever:

> *If I'd have known
> you'd just lay there,
> I wouldn't have bothered.*

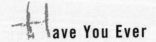ave You Ever

had so much to say
that your mouth closed up tight,
struggling to harness the nuclear force
coalescing within your words?

Have you ever
had so many thoughts
churning inside that you didn't
dare let them escape,
in case they blew you wide open?

Have you ever
been so angry that you
couldn't look in the mirror
for fear of finding the face of evil
glaring back at you?

I stared at Brendan,
trying to find some words—
any words—to express
the terror of those minutes,
the horror of his violation,
the humiliation at his benediction.

But my mouth closed up tight
around the nuclear force
building inside,
thought after thought churning,
the evil in my core threatening
to eviscerate me.

Would you think it a mercy killing?

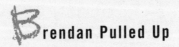

Brendan Pulled Up

at the foot of my driveway,
didn't so much as glance my way

until I opened the door
and creaked to the curb.

Then he turned and tossed the
dwindled bindle at my feet.

You owe me $250.

Would you believe
I paid up?

Stumbled up the Driveway

wanting desperately to shed
the lingering traces of eau de Brendan.

Even messed up, I realized

I couldn't very well go inside and straight
into the shower.

Someone might wonder.

So I aimed for the hot tub, threw back
the cover, almost gagged on eau de chlorine.

But I didn't care.

Steamy water bubbled around me, over me,
jetted inside me.

The monster laughed out loud.

Cleansed, chlorinated to the point of chemical
peel, sore muscles relieved,

I felt almost human again.

Tiptoe to my room, up a darkened hall,
past closed doors,

I wondered if I'd ever feel completely human again.

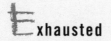xhausted

but too buzzed to sleep,
I pulled out some stationary:

Dearest Adam,

Always great to hear from you.
You're a regular well of information.
Why isn't any of it ever good?

If you happen to see my dad again,
tell him not to bother keeping in touch.
He's a shit and I hope his new girlfriend
gives him herpes. Or worse.

How's it going with Giselle?
(Were her parents on something
when they named her?) I'm sure she
gets high if you're attracted to her.
Have you two done the dirty yet?

As for me, I've got two boyfriends.
One is too busy to keep me out
of trouble. The other just raped me.
I think it was rape, anyway.
Can you define the word for me?
Oops. I think I'm sounding bitter.

Better close now. I need to cry.
(Maybe you didn't want to hear that.)

Love you, too, K . . . Bree

It Was Mean

So mean, it made me feel

    better

but not quite good

    enough

I could only think of one

    way

to make things all

    better

okay, so maybe it wasn't

    truly

the best way to climb

    above

my mounting state of

    depression

but it definitely did

    the trick

in fact, I had to laugh, it

    was

so simple. I

    just

had to open the bindle

    calling

me on behalf of

    the monster.

Close to Empty

We had tooted a lot,
but not an eight ball.
I began to suspect
Brendan had pilfered a bit.

Brendan a thief?
Almost unbelievable!

Conservation was the key
to seeing me through until
morning when I could
give Chase a call.

Conservation, in fact,
might be the solution.

The solution to staying high
and still maintaining my way
through class work, homework,
and family dinners.

I knew I couldn't
manage it straight.

Couldn't manage not to sink
into a swamp of self-pity,
quicksand
for a fractured psyche.

Kristina crumbled.
I called for Bree.

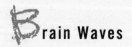rain Waves

              ping-ponging inside
              my skull, no hope
              of sleep or easy

egress

              to a plane where memory
              could not intrude, I bent my
              head, submitting to

shame.

              Why had I gone? What
              had I done? Who would
              want me now? How could I

deny

              the state of my being or my
              part in its disintegration? No
              way to elude the bitter bite of

blame

              I tried to lay the night's
              events on anyone but myself.
              Couldn't. I had tried to

play

              Brendan, and he had turned
              the tables. He was a grand
              master player. I was new to

the game.

The Game Replayed

over and over
all night long,
like a cable TV horror flick.

I laid in bed, memorizing
every scene,
every line,
every plot twist.

Finally sunshine
trickled through
the blinds.
Dust danced in its beams.

The house filled with the everyday.
Footsteps.
Voices.
Coffee. Perfume.

Nothing new.
Nothing unusual.
Nothing, except me.
I whiffed a line of willpower.

Got up, got dressed in
ratty clothes.
Hair unbrushed,
ditto teeth,

I went into
the kitchen, poured
hot black brew
and lied about my date.

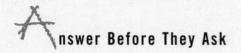

Answer Before They Ask

Great strategy. Mom didn't even snarl
when I said I was too tired to go
to Jake's soccer game.

Once I saw her tailpipe, I called Chase.
Thirty minutes later, he chugged up
the driveway. One look, he knew.

What's the matter, Kristina?

"Too much fun last night. Come inside."
My mom might have accepted the lie.
Chase knew better.

You're buzzed. But there's more.

So much for deceit, for accepting blame.
So much for never telling a soul.
I broke down like rotting rafters.

Tell me what happened.

I told him everything, start to finish,
in minute detail. He gathered me up,
glued me back together.

That bastard. I'll kill him.

I shook my head, tossing tears and thin
streams of snot. "It was all my fault."
Chase grabbed my shoulders.
> *No! Brendan knew what he was doing.*

He pulled me so close it hurt, laid
his head against my heaving chest.
Then hard-ass Chase Wagner cried.
> *Oh, God, I'm sorry, Kristina.*
> *I should have been there for you.*

Stunned

I kissed his forehead,
licked away his tears.
He looked up
and his eyes told mine,

I love you, Kristina.

Eyes couldn't lie.
Could they?
With sudden clarity,
I knew,
"I love you, too."

*Don't say it
unless you mean it.*

Did I mean it?
Brendan was no more
than a nightmare.
But, Giselle or no Giselle,
what about Adam?

*You could snap
my heart in two.*

I thought of the letter
in my room, the one
that had poured from me
only hours before.
If I mailed it . . .

It's bending now.

I shifted
and the throb in my thighs
reminded me of the "new" me.
"But what about . . ."

Come on.
I'm not exactly chaste.

Chaste Chase?
A monster-fed
giggle tried to slip out.
I relegated
it to a tooth-baring grin.

You're so beautiful
when you smile.

He kissed me then,
so sweetly, I truly
felt beautiful, despite
the ugliness
that would always remain.

No one can take you
from you, Kristina.

Tears slipped
from my eyes.
Chase absorbed
every one,
sponging up regret.

I promise never,
never to hurt you.

I wanted him to prove it.
Needed him to prove it.
"Make love to me."
I could feel he wanted to.

I want to.
You know I do.
But not today.

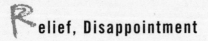
Relief, Disappointment

A flash flood of love and a surge
of need so deep it went way beyond the monster.

"Please, Chase? I have to know
what it's like when two people
really want to."

> And you will. I will take you to
> heights you can't imagine. But not
> until you've healed.

I didn't understand. Go ahead.
Call me dense. "It's only a few
bruises, Chase."

> I meant not until you're free
> from dreams of yesterday.
> When we make love, the only
> people there should be you and me.

He was right. Adam lingered on
my nightstand. Brendan would
haunt me, a shadow, for days.

> When you've vanquished your ghosts,
> I'll be here. Besides, sweetheart,
> anticipation is half the fun.

I could only hope the other half
might one day be as wonderful.
With Chase, it seemed possible.

*Meanwhile, I'd better go before
your parents get back. Want to
go outside for a smoke?*

Soft drifts of nicotine filled my
lungs, soothing one hunger.
Chase held me close.

*Funny thing, Kristina. Before you,
I believed love was making love.
Waiting only makes me
love you more.*

Powerful Words

Strong

        enough to latch on
        to me, bear the weight and

lift

        me, induce buoyancy,
        float me in a brilliant, blue sky

above

        the reach of personal demons.
        So peaceful, in the canopy, beyond

distress

        and self-incrimination. I wanted
        to stay there forever.

Impossible

        of course. Chase drove away
        and almost immediately,

fantasy

        dissolved, like sugar stirred
        into saltwater, as the real

world

        clamped down around me,
        slammed me back down to Earth.

Tried to Beat Mom Inside

but she was right on my heels
as I went through the door.

Who is that boy who just left?

Busted. I had to tell her something,
so I said, "A friend."

What kind of friend?

"My best friend," I wanted to say.
"My only friend." I just stared.

I asked you a question.

Okay. I'd tell her what she didn't
want to hear. "Chase is my boyfriend."

Boyfriend? He's hardly your type.

Anger bubbled. I gritted my teeth.
"I don't have a type, Mother."

Well, at least someone good-looking.

Like Chase wasn't, she meant.
And, "You mean like Brendan."

Exactly. What happened to Brendan?

I was prepared. "We didn't really
hit it off." Understated, huh?

But he was so nice, so polite.

I tried to bite my tongue. Didn't work.
"He wasn't so nice, Mom."
What do you mean?
"He was . . ." I paused, "all over me."
She looked at me without sympathy.
Why didn't you tell me before?
I took dead aim. "I didn't think
you'd care. Apparently, I was right."

Leveled

Have you ever actually felt one up
            on your mom? What an
            exhilarating feeling.

She stuttered, coughed, couldn't say
            a word because somewhere inside
            she knew she was wrong.

So I pushed even harder. "You always told
            me not to judge a book by its cover.
            Practice what you preach, Mom."

Two clichés don't exactly make for deep
            conversation, but I didn't expect
            that (or want it) anyway.

I started for my inner sanctum. Paused.
            "I mean look at you and me. On
            the surface, we both seem so normal!"

Her face contorted, emphasizing every wrinkle.
            "Take a peek inside our family album.
            Like what's in there?"

Do you think that was mean? I guess, but
    it felt so great, it made me grin.
    Sort of sick, or what?

Light-Headed

Giddy from my absolute bluster
(not to mention lack of food
and a big dose of nicotine),
I skipped up the hall,
singing

a Queen
song about paying
dues and doing time, no
crime committed. Oh, that
Freddie Mercury. What a waste!

That guy was really something—a rebel and worse.

In a day when it was supposed
to be okay to experiment
that way. No condoms,
just good gay fun. We
know better now.

As I thought
about that, I had
to wonder: What will we
know better about tomorrow?
Who cares? Hindsight is useless.

Even looking back now, things seem a bit muddled.

Northern Nevada Autumns

are filled with weeds.

Toxic, high-allergen garden killers.
Tumbleweed.
Rabbitbrush.
Russian white top.
        Guess how I spent that Sunday.
Wound up on Claritin
enhanced crank, it wasn't
so bad.
Yank. Think.
Tug. Consider.
        I would put Adam's letter in the mail.
Water. Soak in.
Watch Mom and Scott
drive away.
Bribe Jake to help.
        I would never tell another soul about Brendan.
Direct Jake to dump
the wheelbarrow.
Yank. Think.
Tug. Consider.

I would make love with Chase very soon.
Start to come down.
Disappear for a toot.
Notice my stash was two
snorts away from gone.
I would make a cash withdrawal the next day.
Help Jake finish up.
Send him to 7-Eleven
for Cokes and chips.
I would call Chase while he was gone.

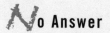o Answer

No sweat.
Okay, maybe
a little sweat.

If I couldn't
get crank
from Chase

who could
I get it from?
I thought.

And thought.
And finally,
one person

came to mind.
I got on my bike,
pedaled over to

Trent's, hoping
Robyn was home
and in the mood

to share some
information. Vital
information

to a person
desperate for
a new connection.

Timing Is Everything

Mine was impeccable that day.
Robyn answered the door,
quite noticeably strung.

> Oh, hi. Trent's not home.
> He went into town with Mom.

"Cool. I wanted to see you.
Can I come in?"
I eased through the door.

> I don't know . . . um . . .
> the house is a mess . . .

It was neat as a pin.
But it did smell like crank.
I suspected Trent wouldn't
be home anytime soon.

> What's up, Kristina?
> Can't it wait till tomorrow?

"Relax. I'm not a narc." I
reached into my pocket for the
semimutilated bindle. Robyn's
pupils went all the way black.

> I thought you'd lost some weight.
> It's better than the Atkins diet, huh?

"It's a helluva lot more fun!"
We laughed and I offered to share
the last of my stash. "Have a mirror?"

> Don't tell me you're still snorting.
> Have you ever tried smoking it?

She was the first to even suggest it.
Robyn the Reno High cheerleader
proceeded to show me a whole new
way to get down with the monster.

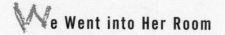e Went into Her Room

Locked the door. Sat on the bed.
Robyn produced a V of crusty foil,
tapped in the last crumbs of powder.

> *This little bit will go right to your*
> *brain and won't clog your sinuses.*

Won't stay there, draining, little by
little. Oh, no. You blow straight through
the roof in one giant puff of smoke.

> *It's an awesome rush. And you won't*
> *stay awake for days.*

She handed me the stub of a Slurpee
straw and showed me how to hold it
just above one end of the V.

> *When it starts to smoke, suck fast.*
> *Hold it in as long as you can.*

Robyn held a match just below the
yellow powder. It browned, bubbled,
smoked. A waft traveled up the V.

> *Here it comes. Don't let it get away.*
> *Oh, God, that smells good!*

It tasted nasty. But it took me higher
than ever before. The monster
pirouetted in my brain.

>*My turn. Don't hold the match too*
>*close to the foil. Crank can burn.*

In seconds, Robyn was flying. Instant
bonding. She didn't even blink when
I asked if she could score.

>*You've got the money, I can get the crank.*
>*For a small finder's fee, of course.*

I expected no less. We planned to
meet up the next day. I went home,
feeling better than I had in a long, long time.

She Forgot to Mention

a couple of
rather important things:

Like how, if you exercised
(riding my bike, for instance),
your lungs fought to hold air.
I huffed and puffed
all the way home.

Like how, when you came down
(I had to eventually),
your head screamed with pain
and your body broke out
in panicky sweat.

Like how your little brother's teasing
(irritating at the best of times),
would set you way off,
make you jump
off the deep end.

Like how parental concern
(inquiring minds wanted to know),
might suffocate you,
might confuse you,
might make you yell,

"Just leave me the fuck alone!"

This Time

it was Scott who asked for
the heart-to-heart. It was a
rather one-sided conversation.

> *May I come in, Kristina?*
> *Can we talk?*

He hated confrontation. I
could play the game two ways.
In-your-face. Or contrite.

> *What's going on? Your mom and I*
> *are worried about you.*

I chose contrition. And feigned
ignorance. "What do you mean?"
He came right to the point.

> *It's like you've become a whole*
> *different person lately.*

Not all of me. Just the Bree part.
Not all the time.
Just with the monster.

> *Did something happen*
> *at your dad's?*

Like he wanted to hear about Dad.
Like he really wanted to know
he and Mom were 100% right on.

Don't take this wrong, okay?
You aren't doing drugs, are you?

What was I supposed to do—
admit it? I shook my head in
hearty denial.

I know adolescence is a time
for experimentation . . .

Oh, yes, he knew. And my mom did
too. Dad told me all about how they
used to get high together.

but I hope you'll think twice before
you do. You've got a lot to lose.

I bit my lip, filled my eyes with
innocence, let it encourage tears.
"I know, Scott. I promise to think twice."

He Talked at Me Awhile Longer

I smiled, nodded, apologized
for my foul temper and angry
words, protested when it
seemed I ought to and
somehow managed
to avoid
GUFN.

When he left, I patted myself on the
back for a game well played,
snitched open the door
and tiptoed down the
hall to eavesdrop
on the kitchen
conversation.

Mom and Scott believed
they'd bitten the bullet.
Little did they know
I hadn't yet fired
off the full
round.

The Next Few Days

went by in a smoky,
crank-scented haze.
Robyn came through,
big time. Her eight ball
looked closer to the real
deal, so I was generous
with her finder's fee.
We got to be good friends.

I would toot a line
before school,
hook up with Robyn
at lunch, hop into
her car for a taste of
tinfoil and tobacco chaser,
stumble into classes
talkative and glassy-eyed.

And just to make things
interesting, I took up
part-time residence
on The Avenue.

Other schools have them too.
You know, designated
smoking areas for kids who
aren't supposed to smoke.   My new friends and I
                                          were far enough gone not
                              to care that teachers cruised by
                              us Avenue bums, researching
                                          potential troublemakers.
                                          Hedging my bets, I did insist
                              on one thing: out there on The Avenue,
                              everyone called me Bree.

Gave Up the Bus

in favor of rides with Robyn,
with a detour or two along
the way to indulge
in some Homework Helper.
(Like it really helped!)

A couple of afternoons she
had cheerleading practice.
(How could she do back flips
and cartwheels
without killing herself?)

Those days, Chase came by
to take me home and stop
by the park for a good long
make-out session.

I invited him to share my stash.
He took a snort or two,
but declined
the tinfoil routine.

I let him get away
with it the first time.
On his second refusal,
I asked why not.

He shrugged.

I've set boundaries.

Meant

to analyze
Chase's limits
that very weekend,

        to learn

just how far
I could stretch
him at the edges,

        to judge

how wide
I might warp
his self-imposed

        morality.

Don't ask me
why I felt the
incredible need

        to test

this person that
meant so very
much to me,

        to fathom

his most
personal thoughts,
coolly dissect

        his psyche.

I only know it was
on the table for
that Saturday until

fate intervened.

Okay, the Air Races Intervened

September is Air Race month
    in Northern Nevada—four
        fabulous days of warbirds,
        jets, and homebuilt aircraft,
    racing wingtip to wingtip,
balls out, around pylons.

        It's a must-see event, and
            we'd made it a family event
                every single year since Jake
                was a tiny baby, snoozing
            soundly in his stroller, despite
    ear-splitting military flybys.

        We always went on weekends
            and I always begged for more,
                so it would have looked pretty
                damn suspicious to say I didn't
            want to go. Besides, I did want
        to go. I just wanted to go high.

So when Mom reminded us at
      dinner that we'd have to get
            up early and dress in layers, I
            cleared my throat as if to protest.
      Instead I asked if I could invite
my friend Robyn to come along.

      Again, I'd made the perfect
            preemptory strike. Mom was
                 so happy I would participate
                 without incident that she not
              only gave her blessing, but
            let me ride in Robyn's car.

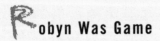

Robyn Was Game

Scott's company had box seats
and plenty of tickets. Robyn got
comp tix, with a can't-beat view.
But that was only for starters.

> *You bet I'll go. Those flyboys*
> *are soooooo cute!*

You can guess what we did on
the drive north of town. We
arrived, diamond-eyed,
behind dark sunglasses.

> *Aviator glasses. Ha! Hope those*
> *pilots aren't as wired as I am.*

I hoped so, too. We sauntered
down the flight line in tight
jeans and tiny tank tops, turning
more than a few heads.

> *You'd think they'd never seen girls*
> *before. Maybe they think we're lezes.*

You thought I was a vamp!
I couldn't come close to
Robyn. Even Bree had to
work hard to keep up.

Wanna give 'em a show?
Have you ever kissed a girl?

The only girls I'd ever kissed were
relatives, and only lip-to-cheek.
Lip locking another female? Never!
And in public? No way!

Come on. It's just for fun. Promise
not to slip you the tongue.

OMG. If I hadn't been so
wound, I would have died on the spot.
Instead, I jumped right into
Robyn's shameless game.

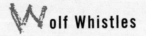olf Whistles

made me pull away,
completely red-faced,
but LMAO.

(You do know what that means, right?)

Okay, my a-double-s was still
attached, but I couldn't
quit laughing.

(In retrospect, it wasn't *that* funny.)

At the time, it seemed
like the funniest thing
I'd ever done.

(What's the funniest thing you've ever done?)

Don't get me wrong.
I'm completely hetero,
and that experience proved it to me.

(I decided that later, when I had much too much
time on my hands to think about such things.)

But seeing the look
on people's faces—some
horrified, some fascinated—
made my day.

(How would you look, seeing two
pretty teenaged girls making out,
right there on the tarmac?)

We Found Our Box

took seats behind Mom, Scott,
Jake, and a couple of guys Scott
worked with. Robyn nudged me
as Mom leaned over, showing off
cleavage to the cute young blond.
He took a good, long look, then
whispered something no doubt funny
and off-color into Mom's ear. She
giggled and flirted and carried on
like Scott wasn't even there.

Worse yet, Scott pretended not
to notice. Or maybe, tied up in
conversation about the latest
microchip technology stocks,
he in fact didn't notice. He turned
the tables nicely when his boss
and Mrs. Boss (in a very short
skirt) joined the lineup. My parents
set an extremely poor example
for us impressionable (ha ha) kids.

Good thing Jake wasn't sitting
behind them. Clueless, he *ooh*ed
at every aerial maneuver. Robyn
and I observed the whole show
(including the terrestrial maneuvers
in our box) with pure enjoyment. It's
always great to watch the world's
best pilots fly, and better yet to see
adults behave like juvenile delinquents.

Three Races

and two stunt performances
        later, Robyn and I excused
ourselves for a trip to the outhouse.
        We hustled off to the car to
"powder our noses," then hurried
        to pee before we were missed.

As we headed back to our seats,
        a familiar form came striding
in our direction. Brendan.
        Attached, as if sewn on, was a girl,
not more than 14, with a fashion doll body
        and child actress face.

Her shorts, cut high on the thigh
        and low on the hips, revealed a stud
in her navel. I thought about
        turning around or ducking into
the swirling crowd but without warning,
        Bree took over. "Hey, Brendan!

Great to see you again," she gushed.
        "Raped any schoolgirls lately?"
He maintained his frosty cool as he leveled
        his eyes. *Can't rape the willing.*
"That's what I've heard." I turned to his sidekick.
        "How about you? Are you willing?"

Still locked to Brendan, she quite obviously
        deflated, and her face paled beneath
an overdose of cover-up and cheap blush.
        "Well, have fun you two. Don't do anything
I wouldn't do." I started away, calling
        over my shoulder, "Watch your back, Barbie doll."

Robyn Wanted the Whole Story

I told her, then she shared her own sordid tale:

*I started crankin' to keep up with schoolwork
around gymnastics, cheerleading, student
council, and other extracurricular crap.*

*You'd be surprised how many brownnosers
get high, and with so much around, I thought it
would always be easy to score. Sometimes it goes dry.*

*During one particular drought spell, I was hurtin'
for certain, and went looking for a new source.
Found him in a casino arcade, cruising for fresh meat.*

*He flashed a bindle and I followed him out to his car.
I still can't believe I was stupid enough to get inside.
He drove east of town, all the way out in the desert past Mustang.*

*After a couple of snorts, he was all hands, all over me.
When I told him to stop, he said, "It's a long walk back,
even if you don't get lost. Anyway, we both know what kind
of a girl you are."*

That stung, but not much. All I could do was ask for more
crank so maybe I could halfway enjoy it. I didn't. He was dirty.
Smelly, like he hadn't showered in days.
And after he started, he got mean.

He did things to me—terrible things, I've still got the scars—
things no sane person would ever do. Of course,
he wasn't exactly sane.
Afterward, neither was I.

Now, You Might Think

an experience like that
would serve as a stern
warning, make a person
do a quick about-face and
sprint in the other direction.

Didn't happen like
that for Robyn.

Didn't happen like
that for me.

Before I Met the Monster

Life had a certain
            rhythm.
                    An easy
                            downhill
Seconds,   flow.
        minutes,
                hours, days,
                        a segue of
                                perpetual
Everything in   motion.
            its proper
                    place, at
                            its proper
Morning alarms,   time.
            kitchen clatter,
                        bus gears,
                                school bells,
Locker clang,   teacher talk.
            hallway
                    laughter,
                            slamming
After-school   doors.
            queries,

                                    homework,
                                              music,
Contentment   TV.
              thrived in
                              repetition,
                                      routine,
                                              familiarity.

ut   Now   Nothing

felt   right

nothing   seemed

proper   but

getting   out,

getting   away,

getting   crazy,

getting   high.

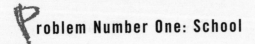

Problem Number One: School

Getting up in the morning,
was it only moments after finally falling
into a state of semisleep?

    Finding clean clothes
    (I was supposed to put my dirties
    in the laundry room, but who could remember?)

Sucking down coffee, nibbling a half cup
of honey-sweetened corn flakes
for a slight rush of caffeine and carbs.

    Catching a ride with Robyn or one
    of my Avenue buds, coaxing myself
    mostly awake with a whiff of white.

Twenty minutes on the Avenue
before the bell rang, tempering
my morning buzz with nicotine.

    Stumbling into homeroom, most likely tardy,
    hoping Mrs. Twedt wouldn't notice
    and reward me with detention.

Making some classes, cutting others,
deciding which would be which
by which was which the day before.

And somehow I managed to convince
myself life with the monster
was not routine.

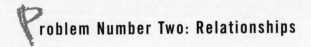

Problem Number Two: Relationships

Old friendships, tucked away
like treasures,
relegated to tokens of yesterday.

New friendships, faulty ground
to cultivate
and build a future upon.

Old boyfriends, a very short list,
abbreviated
further by definition and distance.

New boyfriends, one definite
but distracted,
and no shortage of Avenue wannabes.

Siblings, one too close and curious,
the other much
too far away to serve as confidant.

Parents, ever-present shade, dimming
my sparkle,
kryptonite to quell my bid for superpower.

Teachers, counselors, preachers,
scaffolding,
crumbled by the weight of my monster.

Problem Number Three: Connections

How to get high
and stay that way?
(Coming down was a bitch and a half.)

Finding crank
wasn't really difficult.
Most of my new crowd knew

someone who dealt
(or knew someone who
knew someone who did).

Getting what you paid for
proved more problematic, unless
you went straight to the source.

Even then, things were iffy.
(Stoners aren't the most reliable people.
Even they would have to agree.)

Fronting years of hoarded
allowances and birthday gifts
sometimes resulted

in disappointing returns.
And my bank account
was dwindling fast.

Problem Number Four: Feeling Good

The biggest problem of all.

You know how riding real fast
in a car
or a spectacular takeoff
in a jet
gives you an awesome rush of adrenaline?

You know how spotting an eagle
cruising low over
the treetops,
or watching a baby finally master
the try-try-again
of walking makes you glow all over?

You know how singing a beautiful song
with dead-on pitch,
or getting every test answer right,
including the extra credit
brainteaser,
makes you feel like you could take on the world?

You know how waking up to perfect skies,
enough sunshine to warm you, not
enough to bake you,
or watching a silent fall of quarter-sized
snowflakes
gives you delicious shivers of pleasure?

Somewhere on my stroll
with the monster,

I'd lost these things.

eeling Good

became a matter of scale.
One to ten,

"ten" being one step shy
of shredding the time-space continuum,

"one" being ten steps shy
of dropping flat in my tracks.

Every increment
required meth or more meth.

I didn't have to go all
the way up, but up,
I did need to go.

After a while, even high,
I could almost
make believe food
didn't taste like cardboard,

almost float
down into REM sleep,

almost function
the next day,

almost look forward to my
almost 17th birthday.

Would Celebrate Several Ways

One   with my family. My mid-October
         birthday always meant a

trip   to San Francisco to play tourist
         on Fisherman's Wharf, scarf

too   much seafood, shop Ghiradelli Square,
         and visit my grandma—to see just how

far   she had slipped away toward
         the underworld of dementia.

We   went down the weekend before and it
         was just as I imagined. I knew things

had   taken a turn for the worse when Grandma
         stood up in church and yelled, "I have

to go   to the bathroom!" Flying relatively high on
         the monster, I laughed like a lunatic all the way

home.   Which made Mom mad and made me wonder:
         Does insanity swim in our gene pool?

In One of Her Better Moments

Grandma drew me aside,
put one finger to creviced
lips and whispered,

> *Kristina, dear, I've got something*
> *here I want you to have.*

One tentative hand stretched
toward mine. Grandma's eyes
sparkled, glass under rain.

> *My grandmother gave this to me*
> *on my own 17th birthday.*

It was a beautiful gold locket—24
karat, with an inlay of diamonds.
But the real treasure was inside.

> *That's my wedding picture, there.*
> *And my grandmother's, there.*

Both women wore ivory lace,
simplicity made lovely with a spray
of yellow roses—and my locket.

> *I ask only one thing. Please pass*
> *it on to your own granddaughter?*

"Of course, Grandma. Thank you!"
It felt like wealth around my neck—
a wealth of love.

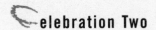

Celebration Two

My birthday fell on Friday night.
>After dinner Mom broke out the cake
>and presents—cool velour jeans from
>Leigh, matching sweater from Jake,
>diamond studs from Mom and Scott.

>>>*Hope you like them.*

"I love them. Thanks, Mom."
>What wasn't to like? I went to look
>in the mirror. The stones magnified
>the pale bathroom light, like my growing
>guilt. Mom came in behind me.

>>>*I wanted you to have*
>>>*something special.*

I watched her in the mirror.
>She reached out, as if to touch me,
>withdrew instead. Maybe if she had
>followed through, everything that
>came after wouldn't have.

>>>*I feel like I've lost*
>>>*you, Kristina. I guess*
>>>*it had to happen*
>>>*sometime. It's as much*
>>>*my fault as yours.*

It was a stunning confession.

And probably not completely accurate.
Yes, she had distanced herself through
work and stretching her affection. But
the monster was a mightier intruder.

*Please be careful.
I'm worried that
you've made some
bad choices. Don't
let them go from
bad to worse.*

Half of Me

wanted to whine.
Wanted to rage.
Wanted to get right up
into her face and shout,

"What about *your* bad choices, Mom?
Have you ever once stopped to consider
how they not only created me,
but helped mold me
into the not-so-fine,
not-so-upstanding,
old-beyond-her-years,
not-exactly-a-lady
standing in front of you?"

The other half

told me to shut up,
told me to smile,
told me to find a hint
of contrition and agree,

423

"You're right, Mom, some of my choices
haven't been the best lately.
I promise to try harder to do the right
things, and make you proud of me."

Considering I had made plans
with Chase for celebration number three,
plans that might very well test
just how bad my choices had become,
guess which half won.

Let's Just Say I Got to Go

Chase picked me up for my Big Day.
He actually knocked, went *mano a*
mano with Mom and Scott.

> *Evening. So nice to finally meet*
> *you. Kristina has told me so*
> *many good things about you.*

Oh, that boy was a player! Scott
shook his hand, invited him inside
and Mom thawed her frozen glare.

> *Don't worry about a thing. The*
> *concert may run late, but we'll be*
> *back before we turn into pumpkins!*

We didn't have a concert in mind,
of course. Chase's mom was out of town.
He had a special party planned.

> *I got the E. It's critical—pure MDMA,*
> *the real deal. But you don't have to try*
> *it if you don't want to.*

Speed, with a hint of psychedelia?
Going primeval, no fear, no pain?
"I want to do everything with you."

> *Cool. 'Cause I want you to go*
> *all the way to heaven.*
> *And I want to take you there.*

We got to his house hours before the
others would arrive. (Parents gone?
Stoner grapevine buzzes overtime.)

> *Let's drop the E right now.*
> *I want you to peak while it's*
> *just you and me.*

I had no idea what to expect.
It took an hour to come
on and discover a new universe.

Ecstasy Is Hard to Describe

It's like

          falling
          softly   floating
          into a   on your
          pool of   back   deciphering
          crystal   circular   codes
          mountain   beneath   in the
          water   vibrant   clouds
                       sky   spinning
                                     dizzy
                                     fast.

It isn't at all like

          going
          clear   throwing
          out of   yourself   hallucinating
          your   in front   black
          head   of a   widows
          lunatic   runaway   and black
          mad   train   helicopters
                       insane   behind you
                                     crazy.

It's a lot more like   jumping
                              into   accepting
                              your own   past   forgiving
                              brain,   failures   yourself
                              ferreting   freeing   and those
                              what's   self   you love
                              inside   destructive   and even
                                                demons   those you
                                                                  despise.

Chase Was Right There

riveted to my side
as I laughed,
as I cried.

Finally, he kissed me,
and it was just as fine
as any kiss
could ever be.
Tender.
Blossoming.
Passionate.
Intense.

Only on E, it was more.
It was like opening
myself up as wide as
I could go, inviting him inside.

He crawled right in, filled me
with love so close to perfect,
I asked him to pick me up,
carry me off into his bed.
He did.

Chase Wagner,
the most beautiful man
in the whole wide world
(despite what the rest of the world
could see),

showed me exactly how
making love should be.

I Was Aglow

at the first knock.
Soon the house filled
    with friends,
    with acquaintances,
    with complete strangers.
            I wanted to get to know
            each and every one.
I wanted them all to know
everything about me:
    my intellect,
    my beauty,
    my righteousness.
            Maybe you have to have been
            there (or to a rave) to relate.
I had accessed my innermost
recesses. I needed
    to explore,
    to expand,
    to excavate.
            The most incredible place I'd
            ever been was right inside of me.
If I left, I might never find
it again, and so I refused

to sink down,
to close the door,
to rebuild the wall.
When someone offered a second dose
of birthday E, I said, "Absolutely."
And when someone broke
out the crank, I was ready
to snort up,
to smoke up,
to shoot up.
I should have been scared to death.
But ecstasy dissolves all fear.

Unforgettable Birthdays

aren't easy to come by.

Do you remember
your 4th? Your 12th?

To my 90th birthday,
I will never forget my 17th.

If you *do* remember
them, why?

It was a day of firsts: giving
myself willingly to ecstasy.
To a man. A needle.

Presents? Surprises?
Firsts?

It didn't hurt, not at all.
The sting was rather
pleasant, like excising
an ingrown toenail.

Or did pain define
those memorable days?

Now take the rush of
snorting, multiply by
100, you get smoking.
To find mainlining, you
approach infinity.

Have you ever once in your life
reached out to touch infinity?

levation

Oh, but a whole lot more. They say people
who die from ecstasy die from overheating.

Adding speed to the mix accelerates the process
because it makes you want to dance until the sun comes up.

The music made me dance. It entered my brain,
firing spark plugs and pistons. It revved me to my feet.

The crank was jet fuel, pumping through my veins, propulsion.
I shifted into overdrive, motor heating steadily.

I danced with guys, I danced with girls, hotter, closer,
melting together like candles in a south-facing window.

Our dance was primitive, beautiful, waves at high tide.
Our dance was sensual, sexual, and yet somehow innocent.

Spent calories orbited, raising temperatures. Some drank alcohol.
The wise drank water. It tasted as good as champagne.

And then somehow the subject of my birthday came up.
Word spread and the mood elevated beyond celebratory.

Gifted with kisses. Tender. Probing. Inviting. Feminine. Masculine.
One emptying into the next, eddies in the swollen river.

I kept my eyes closed, absorbing sensation until it screamed
for release. So the part that came next seemed very right.

Don't Know

whose blade it was,
whose idea it was.

I don't remember
saying yes.
I know I didn't
say no.

The knife was sharp.
One knick at my wrist.
It didn't even hurt.
It didn't seem wrong.

Rust in my mouth.
Rich red salt.
I drank it down,
asked for more.

Offered my own
to those who would partake.
Fever. Fire. I was on fire.
Time hesitated.
Solid earth gave way.
Strong arms caught me,
carried me into the cool of outside.

A familiar mouth found mine.
I looked into Chase's eyes,
found emotions in turmoil.

Fear. Need. Concern. Lust.
And then he said the words
we were both afraid to hear.
I love you, Kristina.

Was Cinderella

and Chase was my unlikely Prince Charming.
(Hey, I'd graduated from
knights to princes, even if they were unlikely.)

Suddenly I was very sure.
"I love you, too, Chase."
                              For real?
I reached up and kissed him and it
was very, very real, despite the quite
surreal juxtaposition of colors
in the night sky.
                              You take my breath away.
"Make love to me. Please? I don't
care who sees." He might have.
But just then his watch beeped "two."
                              No way. Come on, let's go!
Well beyond the witching hour,
Chase hustled most of his guests
out the door. (A few were tied up
in the bedrooms.)
                              I didn't want to piss off your parents.

We wouldn't make it home until
almost three. But the E insisted
I remain hopeful.
"They're always in bed by ten. . . ."
                              Doesn't look like they're asleep.
Every light was on, upstairs
and down, and I caught my mom's face
at the window. We had turned back
into pumpkins after all.

If You Guessed

I was GUFN, two points for you.
Can you believe Chase
was brave enough to
walk me to the door?
Mom pounced.

                "Do you realize it's three a.m.?"
Chase tried to apologize,
said we'd lost track
of time, talking.

                "I'm *sure* that was all you were doing."
Mom lectured him on
responsibility and gave
him the old,

                "We were worried to death!"
(She looked just fine
to me.) What could
Chase do but nod?

                "Well, Kristina won't be going
                anywhere for a while."
I tried to talk my way
out of her anger zone.
No good.

"What were you thinking, Kristina?"

Scott flashed a half
apologetic look as
Mom carried on.

"Don't you know the cops keep
a lookout for kids like you?"

I wasn't a kid. And
I'd never so much as
seen a cop drive by.
Not yet, anyway.

Exiled

to my private mauve island where pretty
pink butterflies fluttered on my wall in
a lovely E-enhanced butterfly dance,
I tried to be angry, but the ecstasy
wouldn't let me. In fact, it made
me take a peek at
things from my
mom's POV. I
mean, we did
stay out until
the cock woke
up to stoke his
crow. Not only that, but we did
the very things she worried
about us doing, and more.
Introspection
would be easy
as a dual-edged
sword. If you
acquaint your
self with your
self, you don't
always like the person you find
inside. I could deal with that. The
bigger problem was discovering Bree
didn't really give a damn about liking me.

I Spent the Next Day

helping Mom can tomatoes.
It was an annual event and I
had always hated the tedious
chore. But the last tiny tendrils
of ecstasy, infiltrating me, somehow
made it enjoyable. I didn't even mind
my mom's company. In fact, my mood
seemed to rub off on her. She didn't once
bitch, though she enthusiastically quizzed
me about the previous evening's activities.
This very big part of me wanted to confess,
to ask forgiveness, request help. Oh, I knew
my bad habits had escalated, and if Kristina
had had her way that day, well, who knows?
But over the last few weeks, Bree had grown
stronger and her argument—that Mom might
put her away, far removed from friends, Chase,
and all personal choice—was feasible. So I
refused to waver from the concert and long
conversation excuse. And when she asked
about drugs, I summoned every ounce of
righteous indignation I could muster and
denied touching a thing except a toke or

two of weed. I knew she wouldn't be
too upset about that. And by the time
all the jar lids popped down on row
upon row of salsa, sauce, and ketchup,
I was still grounded. But at least
Mom wasn't as mad anymore.

urned Out

Burning

        up, coming down,
        I popped three
        aspirin against the

throbbing

        in my skull, and
        attempted a nap.
        I laid in bed,

sweating

        out toxins, the
        last of the E
        and crank,

aching

        from the inside
        out. Could I ever
        shift into reverse?

Falling

        from euphoria,
        I face-planted into
        depression. Hard,

somersaulting

        through your own
        manure. Harder yet
        to get back up without

tripping

        and falling all over
        again. I felt out of
        control, a meteorite

tumbling

        through space,
        tugged by gravity
        toward certain doom.

erked Awake

well after dark,
yanked into consciousness
by Mom and Scott, yelling in the hall.

"Are you blind, Marie? You don't sleep
like that unless you're crashing."

> *She's running a fever, Scott.*
> *And just what makes you an expert?*

"Come on. We both know the scene.
You just refuse to believe it."

> *We had a long talk today. She swears*
> *the only thing she has tried is pot.*

"Like your sweet, little Kristina
is above lying to you?"

> *But what do we do? Search her*
> *room? Have her tested?*

"We pull the reins tighter. No dates.
Straight home after school."

> *For how long? We can't keep her*
> *locked up here forever.*

"At least until report cards come home.
If her grades are okay, she's free."

What about tonight? Should I try
to wake her up for dinner again?

"Let her sleep. If she's really sick, she
needs the rest. Especially after last night."

Okay. Just, please, try to keep
an open mind. And, Scott?
Thank you for caring.

eport Cards?

If grades were the criteria,
I would be in deep frigging dung.

>>Two weeks till "d" (for dung) day,
no way could I make up for how
I'd screwed up this quarter.

And if they were going to start
searching my room, I had some
serious stashing to do.

>>But I didn't dare move, not
for a while. I stared off into
the dark, thinking about Chase.

No dates? Home straight after
school? How could I live without
seeing Chase?

>>Alone in my bed, I could taste
him, embrace him, feel his
skin, warm against my own.

There, as the house fell silent,
I could hear him tell me,
I love you, Kristina.

>>Live without him? They couldn't
make me. *Wouldn't* make me.
I would go to him that night.

I grabbed my "hideables."
Out the window. Down the wall
like a spider, on night prowl.

                    No way to call him to come
                    and get me. How would I ever
                    get myself into Reno?

One way came to mind.
I swallowed my fear
and stuck out my thumb.

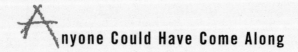# Anyone Could Have Come Along

A rapist.
A serial killer.
Brendan.

Lucky me.
I drew a cop.

The black and white
approached slowly,
crept past.
Brake lights flashed.

Thank God I
thought to reach
into my pocket
and toss the contents
into the weeds

as he pulled to the shoulder,
red and blue revolving.

I wasn't high,
but I felt buzzed.

I wasn't holding,
but I broke out in fear sweat.

Goosebumps popped out like
disturbed wasps.
How much would he notice?

How much more would he guess?
(And how much did guesses count?)

He Got Out of His Car

Evening, young lady.
His flashlight found my face,
concentrating on my eyes.
Kind of late to be out alone.
My mouth felt paralyzed.
All I could do was nod.
Going somewhere important?
I drew a deep breath. Exhaled
slowly. "Just to a friend's."
Do you realize it's after curfew?
I wanted to say something
smart. What I said was, "It is?"
Do your parents know you're out?
Parents? Couldn't involve them!
"Th . . . they're out of town."
I see. Then I can't take you home.
Yes! He couldn't take me home.
Relief segued into apprehension.
Looks like I'll have to take you in.
In? Where was "in"?
He couldn't mean jail?
Tsk. Wittenberg isn't a good place . . .

Juvenile hall? I was dead!
Mom would kill me.

. . . for a nice girl like you.

He escorted me to his car,
put me into the backseat.

What's your name, anyway?

If I told him my real name,
they might call home anyway. "Uh . . ."

Tough question?

It never crossed my mind I
couldn't get out without it.

You have to answer it sooner or later.

"Bree," I said. "Bree . . . Wagner."

Wasn't Scared—Yet

They asked me lots of questions.
I made up every answer,
the most important one being,

        "My parents can't be reached.
        May I call my brother?"

They handed me the phone.
I could only hope he was home.
Brrrng . . . brrrng . . . brrrng . . .

        "Chase? It's Bree—your sister?
        Listen, I got picked up for curfew . . ."

I had rousted him up out of
deep crash hell. It took a few
minutes for him to come to.

        "Since our mom and dad are out
        of town, they brought me to Wittenberg . . ."

Somehow he got my drift. He
told me to chill, he'd see what
he could do.

        No more questions. No tests. Not even
        the rush of a strip search.

They marched me down to a
holding cell, gave me four solid
hours to wonder what came next.

No word from my family. Not
Kristina's. Surely not Bree's.
They took my clothes, gave me
baggy gray sweats, assigned me
a bed in the dormitory.
I joined the general population.
I wonder where that term came from.
They were not general at all.
Roomie #1, Lucinda, was a gangbanger,
involved in a drive-by.
Roomie #2, Felice, was in for wrecking
a Caddie, carjacked at knifepoint.
Roomie #3, Rose, had beaten up
her mother—with the butt of her gun.
Of course, she had a good excuse.
All of us had one thing in common:
a total infatuation with the monster.
Tell you the truth, that scared me
a little. But not that much.

Tough Girls

I spent much of Sunday   listening to them talk.

                    Trash talk.   Honest talk.
                       Tagging   Expression
                          Street fighting   Courage
                             Color   Family
                                      Hunger
                          Need   Speed
                       Crashing   Connections
                    Scoring   Trafficking
                 Shooting up   Popping a cap
              Remorse   Doing time

                  I let Bree do my trash talking.
                  Kristina stuck with honesty.
           Somehow, Lucinda and I found an odd rapport.

             And by the time Chase called my parents
                to let me know where they could find me
        (can you believe it takes a *real* parent to get you out of juvie?)

and they released me bright and early, Monday morning,

I was a tougher girl
with a new connection.

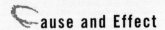

Cause and Effect

The admitting clerk was irate.
She had to redo all the paperwork,
using my real name.
                    She made me wait for almost two hours
                    while she drank coffee and shuffled files.

The counselor assigned to my case
was unsympathetic. He read my folder,
nodding and *hmmm*ing.
                    He told me being a loser was easy, then
                    ordered 24 hours community service.

Scott sulked like a pissed puppy. He
would have preferred lockup to my
picking up trash along the highway.
                    He refused to say one word, and his
                    silence told me all I needed to know.

Mom manufactured a plethora
of tears to accompany her
long-suffering mother diatribe.
                    She had plenty to say about deceit,
                    distress, and sexually transmitted diseases.

Jake was enthralled by the whole
idea of my temporary incarceration,
and the reasons behind it.
                    He wouldn't shut up, just kept
                    asking inane questions.

As for me, I was less than contrite.
Picking up trash wasn't so bad. There
were ways around GUFN.
                    And I now had a direct in with a
                    monster manufacturer.

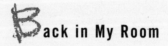ack in My Room

My life closed in
around me. I was
no longer my own.
Mom had poured
through all

my stuff, scoured
my journal, letters,
and address book.
She did find a bit
of evidence—a

crumpled Marlboro
wrapper and a new
lighter. Hey, it made
her day to discover
I was a hard-core

tobacco user. More
lectures, more useless
promises on my
end. She went off
to work on her book.

A sudden wave of
exhaustion swallowed
me. I'd walked through
the last few days in a
total haze. My system

had finally purged itself
of "go fast." It was time
to shut down. I laid down
and surrendered myself
to the comfort of dreams.

Resolutions

I awoke the next morning, semirefreshed.
As I got myself ready for school,
I made the following resolutions:

• One week to the end of the quarter, grades slipping into
    gutter, I would ask for some extra credit work.

• I would help out more around the house, show my parents
    I *was* grateful for the many things they'd given me.

• I would write to my Grandma once a week, even if she
    might not be sure who the letters were from.

• I would reconnect with old friends. And my dad.

• I would finish up the many projects I'd started while under
    the influence—a macramé wall hanging, a portrait of John
    Lennon, a song I'd written about my walk with the monster.

- I would never shoot up again. I would smoke less, toot
    less, keep my bad habits manageable. (Notice I didn't say
    quit them.) I would also avoid sipping other people's blood.

- I would go to Planned Parenthood and get on the pill. Making
    love with Chase was awesome, and we didn't need a baby
    spoiling that.

        The problem with resolutions
        is they're only as solid as the
        person making them.

Other Problems

Mess with a teacher,
        even one that has always
liked you in the past,
        you're liable to get screwed.
                Ditch their classes, they might
                        give you makeup work, but
                they don't have to. I was four
                        out of seven toward screwed.
I tried hooking up with
        Sarah. She was nice but had
moved on to more reliable
        friends. Straight friends.
                Trent knew exactly what was
                        what with his sister, and so
                with me. The Avenue most
                        definitely wasn't his scene.
On the home front, I couldn't
        buy Scott's trust by washing
windows or vacuuming. I had
        zero idea how to turn it around.

Mom, she wanted her little girl
                back. I couldn't go that far.
She wavered between forgiving,
                stern, spiteful, and loving.
I did write Grandma a couple
        of times, lively, newsy letters.
She never replied, but I
        didn't really expect her to.
                Hopefully, I brightened a few
                of her last days. She would pass
                away in January, cold and gray
                as a San Francisco winter.
When I returned to the macramé,
        my fingers struggled over the
knots. I scrapped that project,
        but did finish John Lennon.
                As for the song, I had lost
                the melody and my will to
                find it. And the lyrics brought
                me back to the fold of the monster.

Crank, You See

isn't any ordinary
monster. It's like a
giant octopus,

        weaving

its tentacles not
just around you,
but through you,

        squeezing

not hard enough to
kill you, but enough
to keep you from

        reeling

until you try to get
away. Try, and you
hunger for its

        grasping

clutch, the way its
tendrils prop you
up, your need

        intensifying

exponentially
every minute you
refuse to admit its

being.

y Wednesday

I was starving
for speed and for Chase,
in that order. I bummed a snort
from Robyn, borrowed her cell.
    I made the call with trepidation
    but Lucinda had given me all I needed
    to know—her name, her brother's name,
    and these very scary words: La Eme,
        "Eme" meaning M, for Mexican
        Mafia, hardcore importers and traffickers,
        plus a few chemists, doing their thing
        in desert hideaways. Roberto already
            knew about me. (Lucinda had
            used up one of her weekly calls
            and expected a favor one day.
            La Eme is all about favors.)
                Roberto set up a meet for
                the following afternoon.
                Then I called Chase's cell,
                asked him to pick me up

470

last period, take me
to the bank. (I had a D
in P.E.; what could one
more ditch hurt?)

The Good . . .

Seeing Chase's truck pull
into the far parking lot. Hearing,

It's been a long four days.

Kissing him, knowing better things
lay in store, right up the road.

I've missed you so much.

Detouring to a secluded spot. Gentle
lovemaking, set to romantic sonnets.

It's never been like this for me before.

Riding into town, head on his shoulder,
listening to words of love.

My heart will always belong to you.

He was the second person to tell me
that. The first, well, he had his Giselle.

. . . The Bad . . .

Noticing the letter lying
open on the passenger-side floor.

I was going to tell you . . .

Chase had been accepted by USC—
the University of Southern California.

They have an awesome film school . . .

Early graduation, a full scholarship,
for him, a dream come true.

I'll leave after Christmas break.

For me, a dream or three, annihilated.
I didn't know what to say.

Please don't cry. It's not so far away.

It might as well be clear across the globe.
Out of sight, out of my mind.

 . . . And the Ugly

I was still upset when
we pulled up to the bank.
I was a ton more upset

when the teller informed
me that Mom had restricted
my access to my own account.

Okay, it had dwindled considerably.
But I had to have cash the next day.
You should not stand

a guy like Roberto up.
And I was in serious want
of a fabulous bender.

I'm not sure which one of
the two made me more panicky.
I asked Chase if I could

borrow some money.
But when I told him why, he told
me I was nuts and took me home.

I didn't even say good-bye, just slammed
the door and went to check the mailbox.
I figured I'd better keep checking

it until my report card arrived.
It wasn't there. But something a whole lot
better was—two letters from Citibank.

Inside one was Mom's new credit card.
Inside the other was a PIN.

Did Think Twice

about using that Visa, maybe
even three or four times.
But it was just so easy, like fate
had mailed it directly to me.

Mom wouldn't miss it for weeks.
And then I would deny ever
having laid eyes on the thing.

Robyn gave me a ride to meet
Roberto. He didn't look near
as scary as he really was.
The buy was a piece of cake.
Except for one thing.

Roberto wouldn't deal less than
half-ounce quantities. That much,
straight from the source, was relatively
cheap. And Visa paid for it.

I didn't need it all, of course.
The plan was to sell some,
so my own stash would be free.
Every dealer thinks that until
their nose gets busy.

That's what I became that day. A dealer.
I had just taken a very big step up
in the hierarchy of the monster.

Became an Instant Celebrity

out on The Avenue.
The crank was superb.
And I, being new to the deal,
didn't know enough to cut it.
I sold it like I bought it—rich,
yellow, moist, and stinky.

I offed the half, went
back for more, offed that, too.
My friends were happy.
Roberto was happy—
enough to front me even more.

And I was nonstop wired.
Nonstop tired.
I needed more and more just to get through the day.
More and more just to feel okay.

Who knows how much I'd be doing now?
Who knows how much money I might have made?
Who knows if I would
have smoked up all the profits?
Who knows if I would have
ended up in prison—or worse?

But one morning in early
November, I woke up
and the moment I got
up, I heaved until I hurt.
It might have been the flu
or a bad reaction to Mom's sloppy Joes.

But it wasn't.

Clear Blue Easy

was clearly blue.

But there was
nothing easy

about finding
out I was pregnant.

I didn't know
what to do.

I didn't know
who to turn to.

You've probably heard
that story before.

But until you're
in those shoes,

wearing them seems
so straightforward.

Keep your baby?
Give it away?

Abort your baby?
Give it life?

If you think you
have a clear idea,

try throwing drugs
        into that picture.

                Not quite so cocky
                    now, are you?

So tell me. How
        would you choose?

I Went Through

the next few days
pretty much like
a zombie.

People wanted crank.
I sold it to them.

Teachers wanted homework.
I gave it to them.

Jake wanted to razz me.
I let him.

Mom wanted to know what was wrong.
I had nothing to say.

The monster called to me too.
For once,
I refused to answer.

Friday night, I crawled into bed,
sank way, way low.

Submerged myself
in a world of watery dreams:

Tears. An ocean of tears.
And a baby, a boy,
afloat in that salty sea.

He cried out to me.
Could I swim away solo?
Would I drown saving him?

Saturday

I spent the day:
Throwing up.
Sweating speed.
Shivering.
Shaking.
Tingling all over.
And otherwise fighting
the symptoms of withdrawal.

Sunday

I spent the day:
Throwing up.
Sweating speed.
Off-balance.
Confused.
Weeping.
Tumbling end over end,
deeper and deeper
into the throes of depression.

Monday

I spent the day:
Throwing up.
Eating.
Emotional.
Dazed.
Lost.
Alone.
Finally, I went to the pay phone
and made two calls. One to
    Planned Parenthood. The other to
    Chase.

My Appointment Was at Two

Chase picked me up at noon.
Pale, shaky, I climbed
in beside him.

Hi. You look awful.

I smiled. "Whose fault is that?"
We laughed at the not-funny joke
and headed into town.

Are you okay?

I shook my head. "I'm pregnant,
remember?" I leaned into
my hands, let the tears flow.

Please don't cry. I'm here for you.

Here? He was going off to sunny
Southern California. I didn't need
him anyway. Did I?

I love you. More than I realized.

"I love you, too. But I'm scared,
Chase." He pulled to the side
of the road.

I'll take care of you. The baby, too.

Was he giving me another choice?
Could I make that decision?
I was only 17.

Marry me, Kristina.

My knees buckled. My stomach
churned. Chase had stepped up to the plate.
The pitch was up to me.

lanned Parenthood

was a cinder-block
nightmare. It felt
like prison without
the comfort of bars.

Ugly in orange,
the waiting room
made me want to
throw up. So I did.

A dozen women
gave sympathetic
looks as I returned
from the bathroom.

One by one, they
disappeared as a
stern woman in white
called their names.

Chase held my hand
as we watched them
reappear, one by
one, ashen as ghosts.

A procession of
wraiths, that's what
it was. And I was in
the back of the line.

> I rocked against the
> hard plastic chair.
> Finally the woman
> called, "Bree Wagner."

Chase flinched, then
whispered in my ear:
*I prefer the sound
of Kristina Wagner.*

Already Knew My Options

I listened patiently as the saccharine
Ms. Sweetwater outlined them again.

She did confirm that should I choose
abortion, my parents would not
have to know. All I needed was $500
and someone to drive me home.

She gave me the name of a
local adoption agency,
urged me to consider placing
my baby in a loving home.

And then she asked me
the date of my last period.
Hard as it was, I thought
back to a night up at

Chamberlain Flat, when I used
that period as an excuse to say no.
It was the weekend before school
started. Add a couple of weeks and . . .

I gained a terrible insight.
Chase was not the baby's father.

Brendan was.

The Realization

was like jamming
a paper clip
into a light socket:

profoundly stunning;

like cinching
a garbage bag tight
around my neck:

completely suffocating.

A mad surge
of blood rushed
to my brain,

pounding temples and eardrums

before draining
away completely.
My face went Arctic,

diving deep freeze,

glacier blue.
Graveyard cold
hugged me tight,

rattling teeth and bones.

Chase called my
name. Ms. Sweetwater
skittered to her feet

and everything went black.

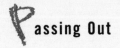assing Out

is the strangest thing.
One minute
you're here.
Then with a mere
cerebral flutter,
you're not.
Part of your brain
insists you're dead.
Of course, you're not.
Another part says it's
better there, in the dark.
Where, exactly, are you?
Somewhere, you hear
voices, urgent.
Could you be in limbo?
A thin beam of light
calls to you.

Will you reach heaven?
                          Brighter now,
                          white and beautiful.
You hurry in that direction.
                          Your eyes acquiesce,
                          and open to discover . . .
you're back in hell, after all.

Voices

	Chase		**Sweetwater**
Nurse		**Doctor**	
	Kristina?		"Bree?"
"Honey?"		"Young lady!"	
	Hello?		"Hello?"
"Heart rate?"		"Accelerated."	
	Wake up!		"Wake up!"
"Breathing?"		"Shallow."	
	Please?		"Now!"
"Here she comes."		"There she is."	
	Talk to me.		"Talk to us."
"She'll be fine."		"She's fine."	
	You fine?		"She's just fine."

496

Oh Yeah, I Was Fine

Dandy	in fact.
Pregnant	by a sex fiend.
Starving	for the monster.
Scared	to admit either
	to those close to me
	who remained
clueless	eyes closed to every
negative	thing about me, or
dying	to know every
dirty	little tidbit.
	And the only one
	who knew every little
	negative, dirty thing
	would have
forgiven	me anything.

Chase Steadied Me

as we walked to his truck,
hand in hand. He opened
the door, helped me inside,
slid in behind the wheel.

So tell me.

I considered playing
ignorant, but knew he
wouldn't let go.
"About the baby . . ."

My eyes unlocked
from his, but not quickly
enough to conceal the truth.

Brendan is the father.

My throat constricted,
like a rubber band twisting
around my admission.

"Oh, God, Chase.
It's all so wrong!"

Our eyes reconnected.
In his, I found sympathy.
And jealousy.

> *It doesn't matter, Kristina.*
> *We can make it right.*

He Drove Me Home—Slowly

My stomach flip-flopped
with every curve and brake.

    Finally, he asked,
        So what do you think?
I had no answers.
None at all.

    So he joked,
        Should be a cute kid, anyway.
Which made me smile
but still gave me no answers.

    He offered,
        Don't answer me now.
Not then, but soon.
I was already six weeks p.g.

    He probed,
        I know it's a tough decision . . .

Tough. Too tough.
And all mine to make.

He dared,

but life is full of tough decisions.

Like a guy would ever
have to face *this* one.

He suggested,

Maybe you should talk to your mom.

My Mom?!?!

The ice princess?   The bitch queen?
The "mother" of all mothers?

What was he thinking?
How could I talk to *her*?

We hadn't really talked in months.
What would I tell her now?

That I was pregnant?
That I was pregnant because I was raped?
That I was raped because I would have done

anything

for just one more taste of the monster?

Where would I start?
Where would I finish?
How much to admit?
How much to hide?

How much to confess?

Where would I find such nerve
without crank to open my mouth?

And if I did dig down deep enough to find it,
would I crumble and weep?

Would she?

The Kitchen Was Warm

and carried a scent
of hot butter, wrapped
in cinnamon.

It reminded me
of when I was little.

Before Jake.
Before Scott.
Despite Dad.

Back when I still believed
Mom was the perfect mother.
She, Leigh, and I were the trinity.

We baked together.
Canned together.
Planned together.

Plotted birthdays
and holidays around
homemade gifts
that didn't cost much
but time and love.

And the fun was not only
in the giving, but
in the shared creation.

I adored Mom then.

Could my own child
ever love me so?

Somehow She Didn't Notice

the wavering tone of my "Hi, Mom."

I sat down at the table and she brought
me a plate of warm oatmeal cookies.

Hi, Honey. How was your day?

I almost laughed. I almost cried.
I managed to hold both inside. "Okay."

Good deal. Hey, I need your input.

My input? Was this some odd
attempt at bonding?

*What should we get Leigh
for Christmas?*

Christmas. It would come right
on schedule, despite my predicament.

*I already put an Xbox
on layaway for Jake.*

Whatever choices I made, Jake would
indulge in the latest video games.

*And I got Scott a new
set of clubs.*

Come spring, regardless of my decision,
Scott would enjoy a great game of golf.

But I'm just not sure about Leigh. . . .

Leigh. Would she ever know
the pleasure—or terror—of pregnancy?

> *Does she have a DVD player?*

I bobbed my head. "Heather does.
How about a Palm Pilot?"

> *Great idea! Leigh's so disorganized!*

The ice princess gently stroked
my hair, and for one very scary instant . . .

> *There's the buzzer. More cookies?*

I verged on coming clean.

I Opened My Mouth

just as Scott rumbled
through the door,
winding down what
I guessed must have
been a very long ramble:

> *. . . out-of-touch politicians . . .*
> *. . . the !@#!*#@ economy . . .*
> *. . . the next round of layoffs . . .*
> *. . . the boss's decision to scale*
> *back raises and Christmas*
> *bonuses, despite signing*
> *off on his own 20% pay hike . . .*

So much for ho-ho-ho.
So much for confessions.
So much for answers.

And then Mom made
the mistake of turning
on the radio as a weather
forecaster announced
we could expect snow,
and enough of it for
the ski resorts to enjoy
a lucrative Thanksgiving.
Scott went off again.

Just @!$%#@! perfect,
with the Jeep in the shop
and the Subaru needing tires.
November snow!
Can you imagine a worse omen?

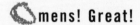mens! Great!

I wasn't about to try and dissuade
the Powers-That-Be.
> I still needed answers, however.
> I picked up the phone, went into
> my room, and made a few calls.

The first was to Dad. Not sure why.
Got his answering machine:
> *Me and Linda Sue were feeling*
> *blue, so we went to Mexico.*
> *Leave your number.*
> *I'm getting a hummer.*

> Linda Sue? Was she from Kentucky?
> No doubt "Miss Louisville" paid for their trip.
> But did the world have to know they had oral sex?
> And who made Dad a (very bad) poet?

On a crazy whim, I called Adam next.
Guess who was whining in the background.

Kristina? [Momento, Lince. I'll be right there.]
Well, yeah, we're hangin' out pretty steady.
In fact—you won't believe this—
I'm going to be a daddy next summer.

Oh, yeah, I believed it all right.
Apparently, though Lince still lacked
feeling in one arm, other parts felt plenty.
So much for Giselle. So much for summer visits.

I muttered congratulations and hung up
without sharing my own "good news."

Thought About Calling Leigh

but figured she'd tell Mom, "for my own good."
I called Robyn instead.

"So I've got this friend who just
found out she's pregnant . . ."

>*Total bummer. How far gone are*
>*y—I mean . . . is she?*

"Six weeks. She's too scared
to tell her parents. . . ."

>*No doubt. What about the father?*
>*Does he know?*

"No. And she's not going to
tell him. He's a real a-hole."

>*No help from the father, no help*
>*from her parents? Only one answer.*

"You mean abortion. What
about adoption?"

>*Let me tell you a little story about*
>*what happened to a friend of mine. . . .*

Seems Robyn's friend chose adoption,
then saw her baby and changed her mind.

"I don't see what's so
awful about that!"

> Ask the adoptive parents. I'd tell you
> to ask the baby, but you can't.

Seems Robyn's friend wasn't really
ready to be a mommy.

"So . . . what? She gave the baby
up for adoption, after all?"

> She went on a three-day bender. The
> baby's crying drove her nut buckets.

Seems, arm in arm with the monster,
Mommy shut the baby up.
For good.

Snow
      Began
           to
               Fall

silent   come
  wisps   dusk
    growing   lovely
      bold   tangos
silver   wicked   wind
  frosted   relentless   and
    morning   hinting   flake
     white   winter's
breath   landscape   random
  taking   reflecting   temper
    dazzling   purple
     lifting   painted
but as   me to   sky
  Newton   heights
    would   I'd
     opine   never
      what   approached
       goes
        skyward
        must
         surely
         crash.

now Day

No plows, no buses,
no school, nothing to do but fret.
I picked up the newspaper.
There, headlining Local News:

MAJOR DRUG BUST
with a picture of Roberto
in a sporty pair of cuffs,
followed by a daunting exposé—
La Eme and the crank epidemic.
Plus, in *Sierra Living*
a complementary piece
outlining the horrors of meth:

How it eats big holes in the brain, destroys
the pleasure center. How it shows up
in X rays as big black dead spots spoiling gray matter.

How quitting is next to impossible
and even those users who suffer
through often never recover completely.
Footnote:

Possible
pregnancy
complications
crank
baby
birth
defects
health
and behavior
abnormalities.

Too Much

to think about.

Too much to bear.
And time was running short.

I knew I couldn't marry Chase.

I knew he would stand by me.
But he deserved his dreams.

I feared closing that door.

I feared the uncertainty
of choosing parenthood.

I doubted I could give my baby away.

I doubted more I could raise it
on my own—with or without defect.

I needed	a solid dose of courage.
	I needed the strength only the monster could give me.
I regretted	my weakness as I inhaled.
	I regretted making the decision to snuff out my baby's life.

Needed Two Things

The ride home was easy.
Robyn offered to drive,
as long as it didn't interfere
with her cheerleading.

The $500, however, presented a challenge.
My bank account was low desert dry.
The Visa was maxed high.

Chase refused to help.
He was "floored" by my decision.
Another option came to mind, one
that owed me a lot more than money.
First Brendan denied paternity.
I reminded him about DNA.

Next he claimed poverty.
I threatened full disclosure.
To his hoity parents. To his toity girlfriend.
To his probation officer.
(A DUI, post—Air Races.)
Okay, he'd cough up the money.

Distasteful as it was to see
him again, it provided
a matchless opportunity.

You sure you're pregnant?
You sure it's mine?
You're not b-s-ing me?

"I'm sure. It's yours. No bull.
Hard to believe your balls were big
enough to accomplish it, huh?"

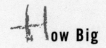ow Big

were
my
balls?

Big
enough
to
follow
through?

Didn't Sleep

the night before,

just sat at the window staring at starlight,

gentle glitters upon a crust

of new snow,

wishing I could wish upon

a star and make it all just an evil dream,

one I could wake from,

but no such

luck.

esmerized

by the come and go,
  the sad drift and flow
of lives in painful transition,
  I sat, waiting for an ending.

  The clinic was gated,
    walled and secure,
  but nothing felt safe
    nothing felt sane.

Why do they make you
  wait so long, trembling
in the shadow of
  fear and remorse?

  I wept, as my sisters
    wept at what might
  have been, had we turned
    in another direction.

And then, midst waves of
  heartache, I felt a flutter
in my belly, no more than the
  whisper of an eyelash.

  Later, my doctor and my
    mom would tell me it
  was much too early
    to feel a fetus move.

Whatever it was, maybe gas,
        maybe God, I took it as
a plea from the life growing
        viable inside me.

                        I would not abort my baby.
                            Nor give it away. I
                        would carry it proudly, and when
                            it entered this world,
        I would be the perfect mother.
            I could only hope
        it wasn't Bree, materializing
            inside of me.

ore Choices

I told you once before
that life is full of   choices.
Sometimes, good or bad,
hard or easy, we make   the right choices.

When I told my mom,
she cried and cursed   my choices.
Then she softened and
thanked me for honoring   my child.

She and Scott argued,
talked and finally agreed   to offer haven
as long as I finished school.
Chase likewise promised   to care for

us, work two jobs if need
be. It gave me even more   to love
him for, but I sent him off
to USC. As my baby grew,   mother love

replaced romantic love,
almost diminished   love
for the monster. I tried
to quit, but my need was   so deep

I did slip once or twice.
One tiny snort was all   it took
to satisfy desire so
deep it snatched   my breath away.

But don't worry.
I swear it was only   a time or two.
You won't tell,
will you?

I Won't Bore You

with all the tedious details
of the next seven months—
the day-to-day grind,
belly burgeoning
around the life
growing
inside
me.

Instead,
I offer a
few highlights,
the top ten reasons
my pregnancy wasn't so
awful, followed by a top ten
countdown of lowlights

(I know that's not a word.
Consider it poetic license.)

Highs

10) Feeling my baby move
    at 16 weeks exactly,
    knowing it *wasn't* gas,
    but something—someone—
    incredibly, remarkably, alive.

        9) Calling Dad and getting
          Linda Sue. Asking her
          to define "hummer" before
          imparting the fabulous news
          that her boyfriend was
          to become a grandpa.

8) My ultrasound—seeing a heart,
    beating strong inside me.
    Having my doctor
    inform me that my baby
    was all in one piece, then
    suggest I shop "blue."

7) My school counselor,
            Mrs. Green, arranging
            a home-study program
            to let me graduate
            right on schedule.
            (Six days before I gave birth!)

6) Calling Grandma, expecting
            a lecture and getting one—
            about how every baby,
            regardless of circumstances,
            is an angel on a special mission.

                5) Scott's losing his anger
                            long enough to teach
                            me to drive. Getting
                            my driver's license when
                            Grandma left me her
                            obnoxious (but mint) '75 LTD.

4) Jake, sharing his Internet
         research on fetal
         development. Did you
         know that a fertilized
         egg, 36 hours old, is
         the size of a pinhead?

                    3) Sorting through 35,000 names
                             in the *Dummy's Guide to
                             Naming Your Baby*,
                             opting for the strong,
                             masculine moniker
                             Hunter Seth.

2) Epidurals. I meant to do
         Lamaze, really I did,
         but I managed to miss
         most of the classes.
         Here's to labor, without
         unimaginable pain!

                                        And . . .

The #1 Best Thing

about those seven months:

Holding

my baby for the first time,
knowing just how to do it.

Thinking

his red, scrunched-up face
was really quite handsome.

Unwrapping

the blanket to count fingers,
eyes, ears, and toes,

Finding

all twenty-four, precisely
where they ought to be.

Crying

because suddenly,
for the first time
in a very long time,
everything felt right.

⬛ OWS

10) Morning sickness. Puking
my guts out as soon
as I lifted my head
from the pillow, each
and every day
for weeks and weeks.

9) Listening to Mom and Scott
argue. About me.
About the baby.
About the odds
of it being some
sort of freak.

8) Trying to quit tobacco
after learning how
every puff made
my baby's heart
stop beating. How
could I be so hooked?

7) Going to school (before
        my "condition" became
        obvious) an outsider.
        Knowing my old
        friends and I had lost
        all common ground.

                    6) Boredom. The succession
                        of little-to-do
                        days, stretching
                        longer and longer
                        toward the longest
                        day of the year.

5) Long letters from Chase.
        USC was great.
        The football team
        was great. Los
        Angeles was great.
        Great enough
        to call it home.

4) My dad's silence. He did call
        once, to confirm Linda
        Sue's tale. Then not
        a word, as if not talking
        about it could make
        the "problem" disappear.

3) Losing Grandma, just when
        I'd found her again.
        A waterfall of flowers
        brightened her funeral,
        but they couldn't disguise
        the stench of death.

2) My water breaking, mid-Walmart . . .
        Contractions,
        uterine lightning
        bolts, striking
        immediately
        and not letting
        up for 18 hours.

And . . .

The #1 Worst Thing

about those seven months:

My steady, needful, forever
relationship with the monster.

Learning

that "addiction" is much more
than a buzzword.

Discovering

how very much it applied
to my "me first" psyche.

Struggling

not to give in to inner voices
much stronger than my own.

Winning

most of the time, gritting my
teeth and "just saying no."

Losing

in those moments
when the world
I'd created for myself
closed in around me.

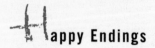appy Endings

I'd like to give you one.
But I'm not really sure
how this story ends myself.

Being a mother is hard.
A lot harder than I imagined.
My baby boy is beautiful.
I sense an Old Soul within him.

But he cries a lot and he
doesn't really sleep like a
newborn should. No lectures,
okay? I accept my part.

I watch my mom with my son,
loving him, as she must have
loved me. She's patient when
he cries. She paces him to sleep.

I wish I could be like that. But
I'm only 17. I feel like life is passing
me by as I stand here on the deck,
listening to him fuss inside.

Sometimes I want to curl up in
a ball and roll away. Sometimes
I just want to die. I only know one
thing that can make me laugh again.

Crank is more than a drug.
It's a way of life. You can
turn your back. But you can
never really walk away.

         The monster will forever speak
         to me. And today,
         it's calling me out the door.

Don't miss

Ellen Hopkins's

Fallout

We Hear

That life was good
before she
met

the monster,

but those page-flips
went down before
our collective
cognition. Kristina

wrote

that chapter of her
history before we
were even whispers
in her womb.

The monster shaped

our

lives, without our ever
touching it. Read on
if you dare. This

memoir

isn't pretty.

Hunter Seth Haskins
So You Want to Know

All about her. Who

          she

really is. (Was?) Why
she swerved off
the high road. Hard

          left

to nowhere,
recklessly
indifferent to

          me,

Hunter Seth Haskins,
her firstborn
son. I've been

          choking

that down for
seventeen years.
Why did she go

          on

her mindless way,
leaving me spinning
in a whirlwind of

          her dust?

If You Don't Know

Her story, I'll try
my best to enlighten

you, though I'm not sure
of every word of it myself.

I suppose I should know
more. I mean, it has been

recorded for eternity—
a bestselling fictionalization,

so the world wouldn't see
precisely who we are—

my mixed-up, messed-
up family, a convoluted

collection of mostly regular
people, somehow strengthened

by indissoluble love, despite
an ever-present undercurrent

of pain. The saga started here:

Foreword

Kristina Georgia Snow
gave me life in her seventeenth
year. She's my mother,

but never bothered to be
my mom. That job fell
to her mother, my grandmother,

Marie, whose unfailing love
made her Mom even before
she and Dad (Kristina's stepfather,

Scott) adopted me. *That was
really your decision,* Mom claims.
You were three when you started

calling us Mama and Papa.
The other kids in your playgroup
had them. You wanted them too.

We became an official
legal family when I was four.
My memory of that day is hazy

at best, but if I reach way,
way back, I can almost see
the lady judge, perched

like an eagle, way high above
little me. I think she was
sniffling. Crying, maybe?

Her voice was gentle. *I want
to thank you, Mr. and Mrs.
Haskins, for loving this child*

*as he deserves to be loved.
Please accept this small gift,
which represents that love.*

I don't really remember all
those words, but Mom repeats
them sometimes, usually

when she stares at the crystal
heart, catching morning sun
through the kitchen window.

That part of Kristina's story
always makes Mom sad.
Here's a little more of the tale.

Chapter One

It started with a court-ordered
summer visit to Kristina's
druggie dad. Genetically,

that makes him my grandfather,
not that he takes much interest
in the role. Supposedly he stopped

by once or twice when I was still
bopping around in diapers.
Mom says he wandered in late

to my baptism, dragging
Kristina along, both of them
wearing the stench of monster

sweat. Monster, meaning crystal
meth. They'd been up all night,
catching a monstrous buzz.

It wasn't the first time
they'd partied together. That
was in Albuquerque, where dear

old Gramps lives, and where
Kristina met the guy who popped
her just-say-no-to-drugs cherry.

*Our lives were never the same
again,* Mom often says. *That
was the beginning of six years*

*of hell. I'm not sure how we all
survived it. Thank God you were
born safe and sound. . . .*

All my fingers, toes, and a fully
functional brain. Yadda, yadda . . .
Well, I am glad about the brain.

Except when Mom gives me
the old, *What is* up *with you?
You're a brilliant kid. Why do*

*you refuse to perform like one?
A C-plus in English? If you would
just apply yourself . . .*

Yeah, yeah. Heard it before.
Apply myself? To what?
And what the hell for?

I Kind of Enjoy

My underachiever status.
      I've found the harder you
            work, the more people expect

of you. I'd much rather fly
      way low under the radar.
            That was one of Kristina's

biggest mistakes, I think—
      insisting on being right-up-
            in-your-face irresponsible.

Anyway, your first couple years
      of college are supposed to be
            about having fun, not about

deciding what you want to do
      with the rest of your life. Plenty
            of time for all that whenever.

I decided on UNR—University
      of Nevada, Reno—not so much
            because it was always a goal,

but because Mom and Dad
        did this prepaid tuition thing,
                and I never had Ivy League

ambitions or the need to venture
        too far from home. School is school.
                I'll get my BA in communications,

then figure out what to do with it.
        I've got a part-time radio gig at
                the X, an allowance for incidentals,

and I live at home. What more
        could a guy need? Especially
                when he's got a girl like Nikki.

Picture the Ideal Girl

And you've got Nikki.
She's sweet. Smart. Cute. Oh,
yes, and then there's her body.
I'm not sure what perfect
measurements are, but
Nikki's got them,

all wrapped up in skin
like sun-warmed mocha silk.
Delicious, from lips to ankles,
and she's mine. Mine to touch,
mine to hold. Mine to kiss
all over her flawless

deliciousness. Plus,
she's got her own place,
a sweet little house near campus,
where I can do all that kissing—not
to mention what comes after
the kissing—in private.

I'm done with classes
for the day, and on my way
to Nikki's, with a little extra fun
tucked inside my pocket. Yeah, I
know getting high isn't so
smart. Ask me if I care.

about the author

Ellen Hopkins has been called "the bestselling living poet in the country" by mediabistro.com. She first hit the *New York Times* bestseller list with her debut novel, *Crank*, and her most recent book, *Tricks*, premiered at number one. She lives with her family in Carson City, Nevada. Be sure to check out Ellen Hopkins online at ellenhopkins.com and myspace.com/ellenhopkins.

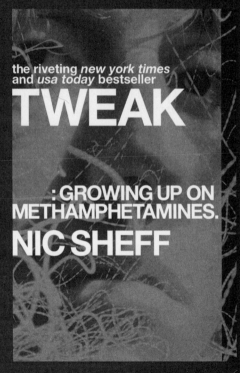

SIMONTEEN

Simon & Schuster's **Simon Teen**
e-newsletter delivers current updates on
the hottest titles, exciting sweepstakes, and
exclusive content from your favorite authors.

Visit **TEEN.SimonandSchuster.com** to
sign up, post your thoughts, and find out what
every avid reader is talking about!

POWERFUL

BOOKS ABOUT STRONG YOUNG WOMEN

HUSH: AN IRISH PRINCESS' TALE
by Donna Jo Napoli

OUTSIDE BEAUTY
by Cynthia Kadohata

ASK ME NO QUESTIONS
by Marina Budhos

THE REMINDER
by Rune Michaels

From ATHENEUM BOOKS for YOUNG READERS
Published by SIMON & SCHUSTER

FROM PULITZER PRIZE—WINNING NOVELIST
OSCAR HIJUELOS
COMES A STARK, GRITTY, AND UNFORGETTABLE JOURNEY

"Like Huck Finn and Holden Caulfield, *Dark Dude* is our street-wise guide to the universe, the outsider with a changing view of what it means to be inside. Oscar Hijuelos knows how to kick around the big questions: Who are we? Who do we want to be?"
—Amy Tan, *New York Times* bestselling author of *The Joy Luck Club*

FROM ATHENEUM BOOKS FOR YOUNG READERS
Published by Simon & Schuster